Wycherly   moment
their gazes locked, hers almost wild with panic, and
his growing sharply intense, as he recognized what
even she did not want to acknowledge. Sorrel knew
she ought to pull away before it was too late. But it
was already far too late.

Then he was kissing her, molding her lips to fit his
own as if he owned her, making a mockery of her
vaunted independence. But to her surprise, he did
not take immediate advantage of her weakness.
Even as she ceased to struggle, his lips changed,
growing gentler, and beginning to coax rather than
demand, until she closed her eyes and surrendered
to him. Only then, in triumph, did he gather her
closer and deepen the kiss again.

The Marquis of Wycherly was a master at the game
of love. Sorrel was a mere beginner. No wonder
that in his hands she was in danger of becoming a
plaything. . . .

The American Cousin

THE AMERICAN COUSIN

by

Dawn Lindsey

A SIGNET BOOK

SIGNET
Published by the Penguin Group
Penguin Books USA Inc., 375 Hudson Street,
New York, New York 10014, U.S.A.
Penguin Books Ltd, 27 Wrights Lane,
London W8 5TZ, England
Penguin Books Australia Ltd, Ringwood,
Victoria, Australia
Penguin Books Canada Ltd, 10 Alcorn Avenue,
Toronto, Ontario, Canada M4V 3B2
Penguin Books (N.Z.) Ltd, 182–190 Wairau Road,
Auckland 10, New Zealand

Penguin Books Ltd, Registered Offices:
Harmondsworth, Middlesex, England

First published by Signet, an imprint of Dutton Signet,
a division of Penguin Books USA Inc.

First Printing, January, 1995
10 9 8 7 6 5 4 3 2 1

 REGISTERED TRADEMARK—MARCA REGISTRADA

Printed in the United States of America

Chapter 1

The Marquis of Wycherly was expected to arrive that afternoon.

In preparation for this great event the entire house was in an uproar. From Sorrel's Aunt Lela, whose shrewdness she had generally come to respect in the few weeks that she had been in England, to the lowest scullery maid, they might have been preparing for a visit from royalty at least, so great had been the polishing and cleaning and sweeping of the last week, the taking up and beating of rugs, and washing and rehanging of all the window curtains. It had been impossible to sit in peace in any room in the house, and even meals had been sketchy or nonexistent, so harried had been the expensive French cook her aunt had imported from London, and so hampered was he by her aunt's everchanging orders and demands for delicacies either unobtainable in the country or wholly out of season.

To top it all, with tempers fraying all round, that morning Sorrel's beautiful Cousin Livia, who was the reason for the marquis's visit, had slapped the housemaid who had brought her the unwelcome tidings that the spring muslin she had intended to wear to receive her noble suitor had somehow been torn in the wash.

The housemaid, who happened to be the niece of the housekeeper, and who resented the amount of extra work Livia habitually caused anyway, had gone off into strong hysterics and promptly given her notice, threatening to set off a major domestic crisis. It was generally felt that the housekeeper herself would not be slow in resigning in the face of such an insult, and it left the harried staff short at so crucial a moment, which was in turn precipitating a near-riot belowstairs.

The author of all this upheaval had, meanwhile, withdrawn to her bedchamber in her usual unconcern. It seemed to occur to no one, least of all the spoiled beauty herself, that she should be expected to help placate servants, or do anything so useful as polish silver or arrange flowers. Her whole contribution to the preparations for the arrival had been to remind her mama not to forget that the marquis disliked oysters, and that she would not be put to the blush by having him exposed to any of her mama's shabby-genteel acquaintances in the neighborhood.

Mrs. Granville, Sorrel's aunt, had taken this criticism in good part, for not only was she extremely good-natured, but she was quite as eager as her daughter that nothing should go wrong to mar the visit and prevent his lordship from making Livia the long-awaited offer. She might, with Sorrel's own mother, have taken the London *ton* by storm some twenty years ago, despite their relatively humble beginnings; and buried two husbands since, each richer than the last. But both of her former husbands had been good, honest merchants, with no particular social aspirations, and she was quite as morbidly anxious as her daughter that nothing should happen to spoil Livia's chances.

For if Livia were spoiled, and sometimes quite appallingly selfish, even Sorrel, who was used to her own beautiful mother, had drawn an involuntary gasp when she had first beheld her even more beautiful cousin. Physically, at least, it was impossible to find a fault with her. She had inherited in abundance the guinea gold curls and lambent blue eyes of her mother and aunt, and her profile was even purer, her mouth, with its enchanting short upper lip, even more delightfully kissable.

It had not taken Sorrel, arriving from America on a

belated visit to make the acquaintance of her English relations, long to discover, of course, that her cousin possessed a self-absorption and a strength of will quite out
of keeping with all that pink-and-white loveliness. If her
mother and aunt had achieved unexpected success, with
nothing but their beauty to recommend them, Livia had
every intention of capturing a member of the nobility at
the very least.

Hence the marquis and the extraordinary efforts that
had gone in to welcoming him for a visit of some week
or two in the country.

Ordinarily, Sorrel gathered, her aunt and cousin vis-
ited one of the fashionable spas, like Bath or Brighton,
for according to Livia no fashionable person would
dream of remaining in the city during the summer
months. But that year her aunt, in a fit of sentiment and
to honor her niece, had determined to return to the
charming Cotswold village where she and her twin sister
had been born. She had even been able to hire for the
summer the largest house in the area, which she had
dreamed of possessing as a girl, when it had seemed to
be wholly beyond her reach.

It also enabled her to invite the Marquis of Wycherly
to spend a few quiet weeks with them in the country,
which in Bath or Brighton she would not have been able
to do, and without the distractions (and competition) that
those fashionable centers provided. And since Livia was
single-mindedly determined to bring the Marquis of
Wycherly up to scratch, in the vulgar phrase, before a
summer's absence should have had the chance to dilute
the memory of her undoubted charms (or before he
could latch on to some new beauty), everything now
seemed set for the culmination of her life's ambition.

Sorrel had never set eyes on the object of all this exaggerated attention, but she had long since developed a
mental picture of the marquis that would no doubt have
shocked her aunt and cousin very much. She had little
doubt he was proud and cold and annoyingly conde-

scending. He would be dressed with all the extrava-
gances of the Town Tulips she had seen in London and
laughed heartily at, with their absurd airs and graces and
mincing walks. His shirtpoints would be so high that he
could not turn his head properly, and his throat would be
swathed in so many folds of cravat that it would look as
if he suffered from a permanent sore throat. His shoulders—unbecomingly narrow—would be helped by buck-
ram wadding to a ridiculous degree, and his coat would
fit so tightly it would require the services of two stout
footmen to help him squeeze into it. To complete the
picture of a vain and foolish popinjay, his hair would be
dressed and pomaded in an elaborate style that would
make him look as if he had been caught in a whirlwind,
and what with the superfluity of fobs and seals and
quizzing glasses with which he adorned his person, in
America he would have been held up to general ridicule
for the painted fop he was had he ever dared to show his
face there.

Livia had unconsciously added a good deal to this unflattering portrait in her desire to impress her unfashionable American cousin. Her own vanity was quite
impenetrable enough that it never occurred to her that
her dowdy cousin in her even dowdier mourning gowns,
was not as properly overawed as she should be, and she
regaled Sorrel with details of the number of footmen it
was customary for a wealthy peer to employ, how many
houses and carriages and servants were considered absolutely essential to his comfort, and the elaborate
method of travel invariably employed by so fashionable
and important a personage. This latter seemed to include
not only a well-sprung chaise with his crest emblazoned
on the door to carry his own delicate person, but any
number of vehicles to transport his trunks and servants
and half his household goods, which seemed to be required to render a visit of some few weeks in the least
tolerable.

Sorrel was sometimes hard-pressed to keep a straight

face while listening to tales of houses so grand and vast that dinner was inevitably cold by the time it could be brought to the table from the distant kitchens, and of households that still included an old-fashioned groom-of-the-chambers, whose sole duties seemed to consist of standing outside whichever apartment his noble master chose to sit in so that he could spread the word whenever he ventured forth to some other part of the house; not to mention private chaplains and majordomos, as well as housekeepers, and butlers, footmen, and pages, all seemingly jealous of their duties and privileges. It seemed to her that such a life must be as uncomfortable as it was ludicrous, and that anyone who would deliberately choose it, merely to puff off his own consequence, was the most ridiculous of all.

The equal revulsion with which Livia clearly regarded life in America, which she saw as little raised from the savages, did indeed break up Sorrel's control over her too-lively sense of humor. Livia plainly believed that Americans never set foot out-of-doors without running into murderous Red Indians or other natural perils, and still lived in mean huts with mud floors and greased paper windows.

Certainly she was not to be convinced on either topic. With stars in her beautiful blue eyes, she obviously saw herself as mistress of just such a noble establishment as she described, with herself, regal and awash in jewels, standing at the head of some grand staircase to receive her guests and happily repaying anyone who had ever made the mistake of snubbing her in the past. It also seemed to Sorrel that she was far more interested in her future grandeur and possessions, once she was a marchioness, than she was in the man who would provide her with all of that. If that seemed to her a perfect formula for an unhappy marriage, she was at least too wise to utter such heresy aloud.

In fact, she could almost have felt sorry for the unknown marquis, had not even her brief sojourn in En-

gland quickly taught her that it was every bit as likely he
possessed little but his title and mortgaged estates, and
was equally on the catch for a wealthy bride to mend his
family fortunes. That being the case, she could only
think they undoubtedly deserved each other. She only
hoped that they would not as quickly become disillu-
sioned, each with the other, as she strongly suspected
they would.

But since she had no desire to remain behind and
watch any more of the elaborate preparations being
made, she had taken the opportunity to have one of her
uncle's expensive and spirited hacks saddled for her and
stolen away on an illicit adventure of her own. Rides
with her cousin tended to be sedate affairs in the park,
with a groom trotting properly behind, which Sorrel
found almost more tedious than no exercise at all would
have been. But then it had been made unpleasantly clear
to her since arriving in England that she was used to far
more independence than seemed to be granted to English
young ladies of quality.

She was growing quite genuinely fond of her aunt,
whom she had never met before. But there had perhaps
inevitably been episodes when Sorrel, by far too independent to be amenable to a strong hand on her bridle—
or indeed, to any hand at all, if the truth be known—was
speedily brought to understand just how different were
the attitudes and allowances between what she was used
to and what was expected of a young and unmarried
woman in fashionable England. In London it seemed
that no unmarried young lady of gentle birth would ever
dream of walking out without her maid to accompany
her, even to do some minor shopping, or gallop in the
park, or go off on her own to view the sights—or indeed,
any of the normal things Sorrel, a stranger to London,
had naturally wished to do.

She had felt compelled, out of deference to her aunt
and in the interest of peace, to acquiesce (more or less)
once all this had been explained to her. But it had cer-

tainly made her wonder how long she could endure so dull and constricted an existence, and she had soon found London so tedious a place she was glad when they had removed to the country for the summer.

But if she had expected that once there the worst of the rules would be relaxed, she had soon realized her mistake. The long rambles across the countryside, or energetic gallops she had looked forward to were equally forbidden, for Aunt Lela seemed to live in constant dread of being held up or waylaid, and was convinced that the country teemed with brigands.

But if Sorrel was finding life in England a trial, it was obvious that Livia found her American cousin as alien a creature as Sorrel indeed found her. Certainly she had taken one look and quite rightly dismissed her as being of no threat, and thus of no interest. Sorrel knew without resentment that she was nowhere her cousin's equal in beauty, for she had decidedly not inherited the twins' pink-and-white loveliness. She herself more closely resembled her father, with her own darker looks and grave gray eyes. And if as a child she had longed to possess instead the golden curls and melting blue eyes that her cousin had so amply inherited, she hoped ruefully that she had at least acquired a little wisdom over the years.

But then she had had all her life to accustom herself to playing second fiddle to one far more beautiful and fascinating than she would ever be. Her own mother still possessed the sort of beauty and charm that made men of all ages, including Sorrel's father, become instantly blind to any other woman in the room. Some of Sorrel's earliest memories were of seeing a group of young men eagerly clustered about her laughing mother, vying for her favor; and of helpful adults either lamenting when they thought she was out of earshot her failure to inherit one tenth of her mother's beauty and charm, or else kindly assuring her that she would no doubt one day blossom and break as many hearts as her mother had done.

They were wrong. Instead of blossoming, Sorrel had

shot up to tower over her delicate mother; and when it had at last dawned on everyone, Sorrel herself included, that the gawky shy child would never rival her mother, it had been by far too late. The butterfly had stubbornly remained in its drab chrysalis, and the young men still swarmed around her beautiful butterfly-mother instead, not the marriageable daughter.

In defense, Sorrel had developed practicality, an unattractive independence and an unfeminine liking for horses and education, where her mother could scarcely open a door for herself. Still, though it might have fooled the less discerning, including her own mother, Sorrel knew herself that it was no more than a defense. And if, in her weaker moments, she still foolishly dreamed of being beautiful and flirtatious, and petite enough to be protected from the least chill wind, at least no one need ever know it.

For one could not change one's basic nature, after all. Young men, when they noticed her at all, tended to be intimidated by her brains and her prickly independence, and would have laughed to scorn the notion she either needed or wanted any protection.

There had been William, of course, though that had been one of the things she had come to England to forget. But despite their engagement things had not been so very different. They had known each other for years, and he had proposed and she had accepted him because their families approved of the match, and because they had shared a real and warm friendship, not because they were in love with each other.

Well, poor William was dead now, and it was only after his death that Sorrel had come to understand that she had had a much more shameful reason for accepting him. It had seemed to her that marriage was the only way she would ever get out from under the shadow of her beautiful mother.

But if Sorrel had signally failed to inherit her mother's fatal fascination, it seemed clear her cousin Livia possessed it in full measure. She had just that same ability to wind others around her little finger, especially men, and if Sorrel knew her to be as self-centered and demanding as a child who believed that the world revolved around her, it had always amazed her how blind the rest of the world could be—particularly the male half of it. It certainly seemed clear that the unknown marquis was as blind as the rest, and trod willingly toward his fate.

But at least his imminent arrival had given her an unexpected escape. Sorrel had spent a delightful morning exploring the village and her mother's old home, and now was enjoying an illicit gallop in the adjoining countryside, secure in the knowledge it would be many hours before her aunt missed her. And since the chestnut beneath her was young and fresh, and the June morning extremely fine, she was enjoying the first freedom she had known for some weeks.

The chestnut, still skittish and only half broken, shied a little at some imagined danger, reminding her that she had best be attending to what she was doing, not rehashing old slights and inadequacies. She let the chestnut have his head, relishing the freedom and solitude, though it was no doubt time she was heading back. The unknown marquis might have eyes only for her beautiful cousin, whether attired or not in her most expensive and becoming muslin; but it would be an insult to her aunt if Sorrel was not there to greet him. She would ride just to the brow of the next hill and then turn back.

It was as she attempted to jump a low stone wall that she came to grief. At home she was a tireless and intrepid horsewoman, and used to going everywhere on her own; and the chestnut, young and wild though he might be, was well within her power to control. But as he took off for the low jump, she felt her saddle slip disastrously beneath her.

At first she was more surprised and annoyed than frightened, for she could only suspect that her aunt's groom, disapproving as he had been of her riding alone, had not tightened the girth properly. Indeed, she was less afraid of taking a tumble than that the chestnut might get away from her and do himself some serious damage.

With that in mind, she tried desperately to keep her balance, but it was hopeless, especially perched as she was in the awkward sidesaddle. She was at first thrown backward, then as the chestnut cleared the low wall, forward again, and the end was a foregone conclusion. She was inevitably pitched over the chestnut's head, and had only enough presence of mind to hang on to the reins, hoping she would not be faced with a tiresome walk back.

But she had reckoned without the stones that unfortunately were strewed along the opposite side of the wall. Her speed catapulted her over the chestnut's head with some violence, and though she instinctively tucked herself into a ball, she landed half on her back and struck her head with stunning force on one of the stones.

Her last coherent thought, before consciousness slipped away from her, was an incongruous one, for she had insisted too much to her aunt on her vaunted ability to take care of herself. *Now I shall never hear the end of it from Aunt Lela,* she thought in chagrin, and then she knew no more.

Chapter 2

The next thing Sorrel was aware of was a pleasant male voice saying encouragingly, "That's it. You'll be better in a moment."

Someone was warmly chafing her hands. In her woozy state she forgot where she was for a moment and murmured with hazy pleasure, "William?"

Then her own words acted as effectively as a dash of cold water would have, and she jerked to full consciousness as the truth came back to her. She was in England, and William was dead, of course. How could she have been so foolish?

But the voice was saying soothingly, "Gently. Don't try to talk. Just swallow a little of this, there's a good girl."

She opened her mouth to object and inadvertently swallowed a good deal of some fiery liquid she took to be brandy. It made her gasp and choke, and she turned her head weakly away in protest, and belatedly managed to open her eyes.

She discovered she was lying on the ground, being held in the arms of a perfectly strange man. His face was very close to her own, and his expression of concern lightened perceptibly as she regained her senses.

Her first thought, even more incongruously, was that he was quite the handsomest man she had ever seen, and would have made a far better match for her beautiful cousin than the unknown marquis. Both were golden creatures straight out of a Greek myth. His eyes were very blue, his profile noble, and he possessed as well a singularly charming smile.

"That's better," he said now, smiling reassuringly down at her. "Just lie still. Don't try to get up."

The command at the moment was unnecessary, for she felt bruised and winded, and her head was swimming unpleasantly, which his brandy had not helped. But she stirred with rising awareness, and said a little dazedly, "I remember now. I took a toss. Of all the cowhanded—inexcusable—! What of my horse? Is he all right?"

"From the unfeeling way he decamped after he had unseated you, I would believe so," her rescuer commented in amusement. "My friend is even now trying to catch him. But you should not be trying to talk, you know. You took a nasty blow on the head, and were unconscious for several minutes."

She put up an exploring hand, and indeed encountered a place on the side of her head that was tender enough to make her wince at her own touch. There was a trickle of blood on her fingers when she took her hand away, but that did not much distress her, for scalps notoriously bled profusely. Instead she weakly closed her eyes again, waiting for the dizziness to pass.

But her continued weakness seemed to renew his alarm, for he said more anxiously, "Perhaps you had better have a drop or two more of my brandy, my dear ma'am. I fear I haven't any smelling salts with me, but it will do you a great deal more good, I promise you."

"Indeed it won't," she murmured, her eyes still closed. "My head is spinning enough already, and besides, I detest the stuff. Almost as much as I do smelling salts, if it comes to that."

He laughed, and seemed to be somewhat reassured. "Very well. But if you will forgive my saying so, you still don't look in very plump current. In fact, you had me very worried for a moment or two, for you lay so alarmingly still that I half expected to find your lifeless corpse stretched out before me."

That brought her eyes open again, for she did not doubt she looked a perfect figure of fun, with her head bleeding and her habit no doubt torn and muddy. He, on the other hand, she was annoyed to see, was neatly and even elegantly dressed in buckskins and topboots, without in any way emulating the fops she had seen in London, which did nothing to make her feel any better. "I am perfectly well, bar a headache—which I undoubtedly deserve," she said more strongly. "In fact, I can't think how I came to be so stupid."

"Oh, we all take a toss now and then. But if it is any consolation to you, from what I could tell, your saddle would seem to have slipped. My friend and I were watching you from the road, you know, and I doubt anyone could have remained in the saddle under the circumstances."

She vaguely remembered seeing two travelers on horseback on the road, but his words brought her upright with a suddenness that made her immediately regret her impulsiveness. Her head began to pound in earnest and she had cause to be grateful for the continued support of the strong arm that held her. "Good God, now I remember!" she said weakly. "And all I can say is that my aunt's groom will have a good deal to answer to, for he was reluctant enough to saddle the horse for me anyway."

"You think he didn't tighten it properly?" he asked. He hesitated, for some reason, then went on more slowly. "It seems the logical conclusion, I'll admit. And yet, at least from a distance, it seemed to give way of a sudden. Had you not noticed it was loose earlier?"

She frowned over the problem, but her aching head made it hard to concentrate. "N-no. But in truth, I was thinking of other things. Wool-gathering, in fact! But still, you'd think I would have noticed if it had been loose earlier. You're right, it did seem to give way suddenly, just as I jumped that wall."

"Well," he said more practically, "these are all questions to be answered in the future. Now I confess I am more concerned with getting you safely back. Does your aunt live in the next village?"

She sat up more carefully, putting up a hand to her aching head and wishing the world did not seem to spin quite so much. "Yes, but it is my horse that I am more worried about. I will never forgive myself if he has done himself some injury—nor will my aunt's husband, I fear, which is more to the point. He is his pride and joy, and I am afraid to confess I had him out without his permission, which makes it even worse. Did you say that your friend had gone after him?"

He laughed. "Did you? Well, I wouldn't worry. The brute took off with the unfeeling speed of all his breed, which seems to argue he was unharmed, and Fitz should catch him easily enough. But forgive me, where is your groom? How came you to be riding out alone, ma'am?"

She had forgotten that foolish prejudice, and since she was feeling both shaken and ridiculous, half lying on the ground with a bruised and bleeding head, answered him more sharply than she would usually have. "At home, where he belongs! If it comes to that, where is yours?"

"The cases are hardly the same," he pointed out, still sounding amused.

"What you mean is that you are a man, and therefore presumed to be capable of taking care of yourself," she countered bitterly. "But tell me, how would *you* like to be saddled with a groom or an escort every time you wanted to slip away on your own?"

She discovered he had a most engaging twinkle in his very blue eyes. "I confess I would not like it in the least," he agreed readily. "Are all Americans so independent, ma'am?"

She was too used by then to having only to open her lips to be surprised at his recognizing her nationality. "I haven't the least notion. Are all Englishmen the same?"

His lips twitched again. "Point taken. But though I've certainly no wish to scold you—how could I?—I still do not admit that our positions are quite the same, you know. Had my friend and I not happened to be passing, you might well have found yourself in an even more unpleasant situation than you do now. You took a nasty toss, and might have been seriously injured."

"On the contrary! If the wretched ground on the other side of the wall had not been strewn with stones, I should have suffered no more than a little humiliation and a tiresome walk home. Pray help me to get up. I feel quite ridiculous enough, and my head has stopped swimming so badly."

He looked dubious, but in the end did as she asked. "At the very least, I agree that it cannot be healthy for you to continue to be lying on the damp ground," he conceded. "Do you think that if I were to carry you, you would feel well enough to sit on the wall that was the cause of your downfall in the first place? Then we can better decide what is to be done next."

"Yes, certainly, but I have no need to be carried," she insisted impatiently.

But she might have spared her breath, for it seemed her rescuer was of a masterly sort belied by his fair good looks, and stronger than he looked as well. He helped her to rise gingerly to her feet, keeping a strong arm around her in case she should faint again. Then before she could prevent him or even guess at his intention, he had picked her up bodily in his arms and carried her to the wall and sat her carefully down upon it.

It startled and embarrassed her, for she was not used to being picked up as if she had been no more than a featherweight—which she knew well she was not. She also knew from experience that she was not in the least the delicate, helpless sort of female—like her cousin and her mother—who appealed to men's protective instincts. She felt an urgent need to get back in control of the situation and said a little astringently, while firmly resisting the urge to hold her head, "My dear sir, all that is amiss with me is a headache—and extreme humiliation. Are you generally knocked into horse nails when you do no more than take a tumble from a horse? I promise you I am not."

"By no means," he answered promptly, for some reason the amusement still much in evidence. "But when I hit my head on a stone and stun myself, I am not too proud to admit I may have suffered a concussion, as anyone else might. It would seem it is different in America."

That made her bite back an unwilling smile. "Perhaps not," she conceded. "But we are by no means as bound up with chaperons and propriety as you seem to be. I assure you I am not made of porcelain, and even had you not happened by to rescue me, should doubtless have been better presently. Indeed you have not the least need to feel responsible for me, you know."

"And what you clearly mean, in your independent American way, is that you dislike being obliged to be dependent upon anyone," he countered immediately. "Are all Americans equally as unwilling to admit when they need help?"

Before she could think of an answer to that—which was just as well, for her wits were by no means as sharp as they usually were—they were interrupted. Another gentleman rode up on a showy black, leading her own blown chestnut, by now completely saddleless and limping slightly, she was alarmed to see.

Instantly she forgot the earlier issue in her concern for her horse. "Oh, thank God you found him!" she exclaimed gratefully, rising shakily to her feet despite her companion's murmured protest. "I hope he did not knock himself on the wall? Is the limp serious, do you think?"

She would have gone to check for herself had not her rescuer prevented her. "No, that you shall not, ma'am," he protested. "Fitz here is perfectly capable of reporting to you on your horse's well-being. Did you feel his knees, Fitz? Is the limp anything to be concerned about?"

The second gentleman, at a glance, appeared to be less good-looking but infinitely more fashionable than her present companion. He looked Sorrel over a little critically, in a way that made her even more blushingly aware of her disheveled state, but said merely, "I could find no cuts or scrapes, so I doubt he hit the wall. I felt his knees and tendons, and both seem to be cool enough. I could certainly detect no sign of swelling. It may be no more than a slight strain."

His friend seemed content with that, but from his appearance Sorrel would not have supposed the newcomer to be an expert on horses. He looked to be much more the dandy than her original rescuer, and was dark where he was fair, satirical where the other seemed open and good-natured. He added, with a distinct lack of flattery, "In fact, if you don't mind my saying so, ma'am, he looks to have sustained much less damage than yourself. Should you be on your feet? Quite frankly you look knocked into flinders."

"Thank you! You have only to add that my habit is torn and dirty, my face is undoubtedly filthy, and I have a black eye forming to complete the picture!" she retorted. "But I confess I am more concerned for my horse. He belongs to my aunt's husband, and is quite a valuable animal. I will never forgive myself if he has been permanently lamed or injured on my account."

"In that case," responded the newcomer with even more disastrous lack of gallantry, "I can only wonder at anyone's letting you out on such an animal in the first place, ma'am! It's little wonder he got away from you, for it's scarcely a suitable mount for a lady. And where is your groom, if it comes to that?"

"That's torn it," said his friend, and laughed.

Sorrel's chin had indeed come up dangerously, for he had sounded predictably shocked and disapproving. "In the first place, he did not get away from me! The saddle slipped. There is a difference. And by a 'suitable mount for a lady' I collect that you mean he is not a rocking-chair ride, which seems to be all that you allow your women over here. And all I can say is that *I* can only wonder why Englishwomen permit themselves to be so hedged round and—and stultified. In America we have more spirit and self-respect than that."

He looked rather startled at this unexpected attack, but rallied quickly. "Oh, come now, ma'am," he said with what she took to be odious condescension. "Surely you will admit that women are the weaker sex, and in need of protection, sometimes even against themselves. I would have thought the present situation amply illustrates my point."

Usually she attempted to restrain the more controversial of her opinions, especially in England. But all of her humiliation at being caught out in such a ridiculous predicament, and her recent enforced bow to propriety rose up in her, and would not be denied. "At least you are honest!" she said scathingly. "What you mean, of course, is that women must be banned from anything smacking of fun or enjoyment, whether they wish it or no. But how would you like it if the tables were reversed? Or do you not hunt, sir? Or frequent gaming hells or boxing matches or go to cockfights—all of which women disapprove of? Suppose we had the right to forbid you to indulge in such pastimes, on the even more logical grounds that they bring you into low company and risk your pocketbooks, your morals, and sometimes even your lives. After all, it is for your own protection, is it not?"

"It seems American young ladies are far more intrepid than our own, Fitz," explained his friend in amusement. "No, no! Don't make matters worse by arguing with her! At the moment I confess I am more concerned with how we are going to get her home. The chestnut is obviously unfit to be ridden, even if he had not managed to rid himself completely of his saddle. And you are in no fit state to be riding anyway, ma'am. The only question is whether you come up before me, for my mount could easily carry both of us for so short a distance, or Fitz goes on ahead and has a carriage sent out for you. For despite all your bravado, he's right, you still look decidedly shaken, which is in no way a slur either upon your horsemanship or your sex."

She had been about to spurn the suggestion that she needed to come up before him, but was successfully distracted by this larger threat. "Don't be ridiculous. There is no need to send for a carriage to carry me no more than a mile at most."

He smiled but after a moment acquiesced to it, if only with seeming reluctance. "Very well, then. If you are feeling up to it, I can't help thinking that the sooner we get you back the better. And if you won't take it amiss, I very much fear your aunt will be worried about you by now."

It was not until he had again lifted her up onto his own patient gray with an ease that made her feel deceptively frail and helpless and strangely unlike herself, that it occurred to her to wonder, somewhat suspiciously, if she had not just been most successfully outmaneuvered.

But as he mounted behind her he gave her so charming a smile that she concluded she must surely be mistaken. Handsome men, in her experience, tended to be like her cousin: far too spoiled and shallow to be capable of such strategic guile—at least in another's behalf.

It was only afterward, when it was far too late, that she was to remember with some bitterness that basic and uncharacteristic error in judgment on her part, and wonder how she could have been so blind.

Chapter 3

As it was, the ride back, even with his strong arm still about her, taxed her strength more than she wished to admit.

Once his friend Fitz had remounted his showy black and taken the chestnut in tow, they set off, and Sorrel had to acknowledge that she still felt shaky and unlike her normal competent self. Her aching head felt surprisingly heavy and it was tempting to let it rest upon the broad shoulder so invitingly near. It was a temptation she resolutely refused to give in to, and instead held it determinedly upright, along with her spine, and tried to behave as though it were the usual thing to be held so very close in a strange man's arms.

To hide her embarrassment and lingering weakness, both of which she despised, she said stiffly, "I believe I have not yet—thanked you—both of you—for coming to my rescue."

He smiled down at her in a way she was coming to know, for his good-looking face held amusement, and sympathy, and an indefinable charm that was becoming harder and harder for her to resist. "No, no, don't spoil it," he said. "You have until now been delightfully outspoken, with a very proper disregard for our exaggerated male sensibilities, and I beg you won't feel obliged to give in to false propriety at this late date. You are not in the least grateful, confess it, ma'am. You clearly hate like the devil being obliged to find yourself in need of rescue, and your pride is almost as badly bruised as your head. You are feeling shaken and out of sorts, and your head aches abominably, and it is only natural that you should take it out on us, for catching you at such a disadvantage. I beg you will not consider our feelings in the least, ma'am."

She almost smiled at his nonsense, but said more naturally, "Well, I confess I dislike being made to feel—weak and foolish. But I hope I am not so—so proud and disagreeable that I cannot accept help when it is necessary."

"Why, so do I, ma'am," he said in amusement. "But I have discovered human nature is such that we are often least grateful for that we should be most grateful for. I fear I am much the same case, you know."

"That at least is true," put in his friend Fitz dryly. "For all his apparent good nature, I have known Guy here snap acquaintances' heads off for no more than inquiring how he was feeling. I understand the army doctors grew used to having objects thrown at their heads if they were reluctant to pronounce him fit again and ready to fight in a dozen campaigns."

She looked up quickly at the handsome face so close to her own. "You were in the army?" she asked in some surprise.

"Why yes, until very recently. But Fitz exaggerates, as usual. I only once threw a basin at a doctor's head, and that was only because he had the temerity to tell me I must remain bedfast for another month at least, for no more than a flesh wound."

The fact that he had been a soldier somehow merely cemented her good opinion of him, and she smiled up at him quite spontaneously for the first time. "In that case, he undoubtedly deserved it! Was he right, by the way?" she asked curiously.

It was again Fitz who answered. "Oh, undoubtedly. Nevertheless Guy was up within the week, and returned to his regiment within two." But he was staring at her in a startled way that Sorrel could not understand, as if he had never seen her before.

Her rescuer—Guy—was also looking down at her in warm approval, for some reason. But he protested at that. "Nonsense! He would have had me invalided out, and sent home, for no more than a hole in the shoulder."

"And you would have missed all the fun," she said, every bit as dryly as his friend.

He laughed outright at that. "Precisely, ma'am. I see we understand one another perfectly."

"Except that I have no excuse for my bad manners but temper," she conceded ruefully. "And a dislike—as you say—of being made to feel ridiculous. You must know my—my habit of riding out without an escort has worried my aunt, and now she will be even more convinced that the wilds of Worcestershire are unsafe, and insist upon plaguing me with a groom wherever I go. Which reminds me. Perhaps you can tell me, sir, why in so civilized a country, everyone is so very preoccupied with safety? My aunt felt more alarm in traveling some six hours from London than I would have in venturing into the wilderness back home. It is most odd."

He burst out laughing. She liked the sound of his laughter, which had not an ounce of sophistication or the fashionable titter she was becoming used to in it, and rumbled most pleasantly against her back and shoulder. "I don't know!" he confessed. "But it does seem that you are right, ma'am. I have noticed it myself since returning. At any rate, I feel very sure by now that you at least are untroubled by thoughts of being waylaid by highwaymen or footpads. But then I daresay you are used to facing off Indians whenever you venture out-of-doors, and so must think my poor country tame indeed."

"That is certainly the general opinion that I meet with everywhere here," she agreed dryly. "For a former colony the English seem alarmingly ignorant about my country." She hesitated, then asked, with a slight cooling in her voice that she could not prevent, "I take it you were not part of the recent war in America, sir?"

He smiled down at her as if he recognized both the cooling and the reason for it. "No, I am glad to say I was not. A most ill-managed affair, though I daresay I should not say it. I am only glad it did not manage to give you a distaste for England, ma'am."

She relaxed a little. "But then my aunt is English, and my own mother as well," she admitted. "I don't hold England to blame, if that is what you fear. It was a foolish war, on both sides I believe."

Fitz had dropped back slightly with the limping chestnut, since they could not all go abreast, and Sorrel was grateful, for she found it easier to converse without his hampering presence. "Why, I am glad to hear you say so," the one called Guy said frankly. "I had many friends who fought in it, and they seem one in their opinion that we should never have been at war with America."

"No, though the late revolution—rebellion I believe you call it over here—still seems to rankle with some English I have met. But perhaps now we are even, and can each get on with our respective lives in peace."

"You are generous. May I ask where is your home in America?"

"Annapolis. Near to Washington," she answered and left it at that.

"Ah." There was a wealth of understanding in his voice. "Then I do indeed understand, and must be grateful you don't hold all English to blame for the atrocities that were committed there. I believe they burned your capital completely."

She did not wish to speak of it, even yet. "Yes, but only in retaliation for our side having burned some Canadian towns," she said truthfully. "And war is never pretty, as I think you must know yourself, sir."

"Yes," he agreed ruefully. "None better. As I said, I have many friends who fought in America, and they seem uniformly of the opinion that it was a foolish war, on more counts than one. For one thing, it removed some of our crack regiments from the Peninsula at a time we most needed them. Besides, War of Independence or no, I will always think America and England to be united, in common roots and interest, if nothing else. We have no business fighting one another."

They were both silent for some minutes after that, each no doubt with his own unwelcome thoughts. For herself she had no wish to be reminded of that dark and frightening time, and some of the sights she had seen; and doubtless he had his own similar memories. And all of it seemed a million miles away from this green and peaceful land.

Besides, he spoke so much like an honest, sensible man, with none of the fashionable airs she had come to expect in England, that she could not help liking him. He also suited her notions of what a man should look like, for he was tall and well built, and from his easy lifting of her, surprisingly strong. Though he was better-looking than she strictly liked, at least he seemed to have no touch of the dandy about him, or attempt to use his good looks to his advantage. And there could be no denying that he possessed a singularly charming smile. She thought him worth a dozen mincing marquis.

At last he smiled and tactfully changed the subject. "And what do you think of my country?" he asked. "I gather it has not wholly met with your approval?"

"Why, as to that, I am sure it is very beautiful, and I am glad I have seen it," she answered frankly. "It has been good to see my mother's old home, as well, for she grew up around here, you know. And I have quite fallen in love with my aunt, for all her oddities. But as I fear you have already guessed, I shall never resign myself to the rules and regulations that seem to hedge your lives round—especially if you are a young and unmarried woman."

"Why, are they so very excessive, ma'am?"

"Enough that I have been in almost continuous disgrace since I arrived. I am forever offending my aunt by going off on my own exploring. At home I am used to going pretty much where I please, but I was speedily brought to see that it is not the same here. I wished to see the sights of London, and neither my aunt nor my cousin were at all interested in trailing around visiting the tower and the Exeter Exchange, so it seemed natural to me that I should spare them what they so much disliked. But the day that I walked from Mayfair to St. Peter's, *and* back again, unescorted, and thoroughly enjoyed myself doing it, you'd have thought I had committed a crime of some sort, so shocked was my aunt. Yes, you may laugh now, but it was not very funny at the time, I can promise you. I quickly discovered that my cousin does not so much as step out to buy a length of ribbon without a footman or her maid in attendance. If I were to live under such restrictions for long, I am sure I should soon go mad."

"It does seem very hard," he agreed sympathetically. "I have been abroad for a good many years, of course. And compared with the Spanish, the English are positively liberal. I take it things are very different in America? Is that why you took your uncle's horse without permission, and—er—slipped away this afternoon?"

His understanding amusement somehow robbed his words of all offense, though she had not realized she had revealed quite so much. After a moment she answered ruefully, "That, and for a still more unworthy reason, I'm reluctant to admit. My aunt and my cousin are expecting an—important guest this afternoon, and I have heard so much of him already that I have grown sick of the sound of his name."

"Why that is very bad, certainly." He still sounded amused, his chest rumbling pleasantly against her when he spoke. In fact, it was growing more difficult to remain stubbornly upright all the time. "What has this unknown visitor done to incur your disapproval, ma'am?"

"Nothing. I have never even laid eyes on him. But I

should perhaps explain that he is a marquis, which in England seems to explain all."

Fitz, a few paces behind, choked for some reason and began to cough, but his friend ignored him. "Ah, I begin to see," he said again. "Do I take it you object to all titles on mere democratic principles?"

She shrugged. "I am an American, after all. Whereas you English seem to hold them in exaggerated awe. But from all I have been able to tell, this particular marquis might just as well be deaf, blind, imbecile and halt in one leg, and he would meet with the same welcome. Your worth in this country would seem to matter much less than your pocketbook, and both still less than a mere accident of birth."

There was another choke from behind them, but Guy said merely, with an effort to keep a straight face, "You are severe, ma'am."

"Perhaps. But I would prefer that to—to—*toad eating* a man for no other reason than that his grandfather bought a title two generations ago, or his ancestors did some trifling favor for a monarch."

"Why, spoken like a true American. But I agree with you, in the main. In fact, my friend was saying something of the very same to me just before we met you."

That surprised her, for his friend Fitz seemed the sort of conventional Englishman to revere all titles. But Guy went on, clearly teasing her, "But do you have any reason to think this particular marquis is either—er—deaf, blind, imbecile or halt in one leg?"

"No, and I daresay I would like him better if he were," she retorted. "I have it on the best of authority that he is something far worse, in my estimation. He is a *dandy*!"

He laughed. "I can see I must visit America some time. But I must warn you that Fitz here does not share that prejudice, at least, for he fondly aspires to that class. Unsuccessfully, for the most part, I might add, for it is generally considered that his tailor makes him."

He had raised his voice a little, and his friend responded predictably. "Well, I'd rather be called a dandy, than a da—demned Captain Hackum who looks as if he dresses all by guess!" put in Fitz indignantly. "Pay no heed to him, ma'am. He is merely jealous. And though I must say I find a good many of your notions wholly absurd, I agree that we make far too much of our peers. That is at least one thing America has over this country, for you've done away with 'em completely, so I'm told."

There was an undercurrent of raillery going on between them that she found rather amusing. But Guy refused to be drawn, saying merely, "And yet I believe you said your mother was English, ma'am? Does she share your democratic zeal?"

Sorrel thought briefly of her gay, beautiful mother, who cared nothing for politics. "Perhaps not so much, for she was indeed born in England. But from anything I've ever heard, she might have married a title herself, for she and my aunt seem to have taken what you call the *ton* by storm, so long ago, though their origins were humble enough. She chose instead my father, who had neither title nor much wealth to recommend him, and was an American besides. And I don't think she ever regretted her choice."

"She was clearly as strong-minded as you are yourself. I would enjoy hearing more of your somewhat novel views, but here is the village already. You will have to direct us to your aunt's house."

Sorrel was astonished at how quickly the distance had been covered, and rather sorry to think she was unlikely ever to meet her pleasant rescuer again. She longed to ask his name, but did not quite care to, since he did not volunteer the information.

But she gave them directions to her aunt's house, which stood at the end of the long village street next to the church, then asked curiously, "Do you live nearby, sir?"

"No, my friend and I are visiting friends locally," he said, and left it at that.

It was not long before they reached the gates of Campden House and turned into the short drive. Sorrel would have directed them to the stables, where she hoped to slip into the house undetected; but as she had noticed before, her rescuer seemed to be of a somewhat dictatorial disposition. He wholly ignored her and continued calmly up to the carriage sweep before the house.

There they came to a halt, and he said again, teasingly, "Well, I wish you joy of your marquis, ma'am. I hope he will not prove quite as bad as you are expecting."

Before she could answer him, the front door unexpectedly flew open, and both Sorrel's aunt and her cousin tumbled out, amazement to be read clearly in their faces.

Chagrined to be caught out in such a ridiculous position after all her boasting, Sorrel was just composing an explanation to excuse her disappearance and subsequent disheveled reappearance, when her cousin Livia forestalled her. "Cousin Sorrel! *Lord Wycherly*—?" She exclaimed in the liveliest astonishment.

She was looking between them, surprise and a growing displeasure on her beautiful face. But even then Sorrel was woefully slow to take in the enormity of what she had done.

And when she did at last, she could have cursed herself for being such a fool.

Chapter 4

Sorrel had immediately stiffened, but her rescuer—the Marquis of Wycherly—said in her ear before she could speak, "So your name is Sorrel? I like it. As refreshing and unusual as you are."

She cast him a burning glance of shock and accusation, still scarcely able to take in what this pleasant, unassuming traveler, arriving on horseback without a footman or trunk in attendance, could have to do with the picture she had built up in her mind of the unknown marquis, all airs and pretension.

She encountered so much amusement and unexpected understanding in his handsome face that for a moment she was shaken. "I'm sorry," he added softly, still for her ears alone. "I shouldn't have teased you. But you must admit it was almost irresistible."

She was in no mood to admit any such thing, but there was time for no more, for her aunt was upon them by then. "Sorrel?" she exclaimed in bewilderment. "Lord Wycherly?" She was out of breath from hurrying and looked, for some reason, more distracted than usual and even faintly alarmed. "What has happened? You could have knocked me over with a feather when I chanced to look out of the drawing room window and saw you riding up together. We thought you laid safely down upon your bed."

Cousin Livia had remained in the doorway, but now she said mockingly. "It appears we were wrong, Mama. In fact, we should have known she had taken the opportunity to steal away again. On Walter's new chestnut, too. I begin to think there is more to my little American cousin than I had thought."

Aunt Lela ignored that, as she did much of her daughter's unpleasantness. She still possessed the remnants of the great beauty that had won her two husbands, each richer than the last. But whereas Sorrel's own mother still looked scarcely a day older than when her husband had brought her in triumph to America, Aunt Lela had grown a trifle stout over the years, and had, so she frankly admitted herself, given up the struggle against encroaching time. She had always been the more practical and down to earth of the two, and was also exceedingly good-natured, as Sorrel had discovered. Where Laura, the younger twin, held sway through soft words and an irresistible charm, Aunt Lela seemed to take a more direct route. She was alternately funny and unexpectedly shrewd, and Sorrel had grown very fond of her in the few weeks she had known her.

"But what has happened?" she repeated, her voice sharpening as she took in her niece's disheveled appearance. "Never tell me there has been an *accident*?"

It was the marquis who answered her calmly, as he dismounted and went to shake hands with his hostess. "Pray do not distress yourself, ma'am. Your niece took a tumble from her horse, and was briefly knocked unconscious. It was lucky we happened to be by at the time, but I believe she is not much hurt, save for a bump on the head."

Far from being comforted, her aunt looked even more alarmed at this news. It was Cousin Livia's silvery laughter that unexpectedly sounded. "Then *that* explains her extremely odd appearance," she said. "I am glad to have at least *one* mystery cleared up."

"Oh dear, oh dear, as if that mattered," exclaimed Aunt Lela, sounding unusually flustered. "Not that I am not forever warning her about—but I don't mean to scold, especially at such a time as this. Perhaps you had best lift her down and carry her into the house, my lord, for she does look faint, poor child."

This was obviously less to Livia's liking, and even Aunt Lela seemed to feel, on second thought, that perhaps one did not ask a marquis to perform so menial a task. "That is—perhaps James, the footman—" she corrected herself hurriedly. "And a doctor must be sent for at once, of course. Oh, dear me! I am sure nothing would surprise me today. And Mr. FitzSimmons, too. We weren't expecting you both until this afternoon."

But the marquis had already quietly lifted Sorrel down from the saddle. He would undoubtedly have followed the second part of her aunt's instructions as well, but as soon as he had set her on her feet, Sorrel quickly forestalled him. "No, no! I am perfectly capable of walking on my own," she insisted stiffly, refusing to meet his eyes.

He took a look at her outraged expression and did not press it, and for once her cousin Livia actually came to her rescue. "Pray don't *fuss*, Mama. You know how much Sorrel dislikes it. Let us go indoors, all of us. I am sure Lord Wycherly and Mr. FitzSimmons must think they have stumbled into Bedlam, for on top of everything else there is no point in keeping them standing upon the doorstep."

"Lord yes," said her hapless mama. "Where have my wits gone abegging? Come in, come in, do! I must confess I certainly never expected you to arrive on horseback, like a pair of Gypsies, though it's lucky for my niece that you did. Where is your baggage? And surely you did not ride all the way from London, my lord?"

She sounded as horrified as if she had said "the moon," and the marquis answered in amusement, "No, no, it is not as bad as that, ma'am. Merely my curricle needed some slight repair at our last halt, and rather than kick our heels for some hours waiting for it to be repaired, we decided to hire horses and come on. The baggage should be arriving later. I hope it has not put you to any inconvenience?"

Her aunt was naturally quick to repudiate such a suggestion. "And I am sure it makes no difference to me how you came, though to be jogging along on horseback is not a thing I've taken to, nor ever shall," she said, plainly thinking that the odd whims of the nobility must be overlooked. "But I'm sure you must be exhausted, both of you. Come in, come in! As my daughter says, I can't think what you must be thinking of us, and I assure you I had a very different welcome planned for you. And if I haven't gone and forgotten my niece in all the confusion, who must be well-nigh to fainting while I rattle on. Why, where has she gone to?" she added in surprise, looking around her as if her words could somehow conjure her up.

"While you were arguing whether she should be carried or not, she slipped in the house on her own," pointed out Livia in some triumph. "I told you she hated to be fussed over."

Her mother exclaimed, but Livia, managing to throw off her momentary displeasure, tucked a hand in each of her admirer's arms, and said gaily, "Never mind! She is the oddest creature, you know. She had Mama in flat despair in London, for she was forever going off on her own, returning as often as not dirty and exhausted, like today, with a tale of having gone to visit some monument or other. But come in! You can't know how glad I am to see you both, for I swear I was close to dying of boredom. I will never understand what people find to amuse them in the country." She gave her silvery laugh again and led them toward the house.

She was indeed extremely beautiful, from the top of her glowing golden locks, to the tip of her elegant feet. It was no wonder most men in her presence tended to forget themselves and stare foolishly, as Mr. FitzSimmons was doing now.

Sorrel, able from the vantage point of her bedchamber

window which overlooked the carriage drive, to take in
the way both gentlemen were regarding her in evident
admiration, quietly withdrew and went to change her
filthy habit.

She was bitterly angry, humiliated, hurt, and disappointed, in roughly equal amounts. It was not enough
that the marquis must have guessed at once who she
was, and deliberately encouraged her to make a fool of
herself. What hurt more was that she had genuinely liked
him, while he had obviously told her nothing but a farrago of lies and had amused himself at her expense. A
soldier indeed!

She was almost as angry with herself. It was unlike
her to blurt out so much to chance-met strangers, and she
saw that she should have suspected who they were long
since. She had admittedly expected not two gentlemen
but one, and for him to arrive in a private chaise, not on
horseback. Those, on top of a bump on the head and the
unaccustomed brandy might have much to do with her
folly. But that did not excuse the things she had said.

Nor could she understand where Mr. FitzSimmons fit
in. She had not known he had been invited as well.

But if, despite everything else, she still was having
difficulty connecting the snobbish fop of her imaginings
with the sensible man she had taken him for, that was
likely the greatest folly of all. She had liked him better
than she thought she would, but he was all but betrothed
to her beautiful cousin. And it would do her well not to
ever allow herself to forget it.

Then she caught sight of her reflection in the mirror,
and had to bite back a bitter laugh. Even when her face
was not pale and smudged with mud, with a streak of
blood down one cheek, and her habit not filthy and
creased and her hair coming down untidily, she knew
she was in little danger of being allowed to forget it. The
Marquis of Wycherly was unlikely to have eyes to spare
for anyone but her beautiful cousin.

Sorrel had scarcely changed out of her habit and

washed her face and tidied her hair when her aunt came
rushing in her usual impetuous fashion, having seen her
guests suitably disposed. Sorrel unconsciously steeled
herself for a scold, but it quickly became apparent that
her aunt was too much torn between triumph at the marquis's arrival and concern for her niece to think of scold-
ing her. "Dearest, are you all right?" she exclaimed, her
cheeks pink with exertion and the effects of the hot afternoon. "You should have allowed Lord Wycherly to
carry you up, for you still look alarmingly pale. And
only to think of its being him to rescue you. You could
have knocked me over with a feather, like I said, when I
chanced to glance out the window, and saw you riding
up together."

Sorrel, who had no desire to discuss the marquis with
her aunt, hastened to assure her that nothing was amiss
but a slight headache.

Her aunt sank gratefully into a chair, fanning herself.
"Well, that's a blessing, at least." But she could not remain off her favorite subject for long. "But only tell me,
my love, what did you think of him?" she demanded ex-
citedly. "Isn't he the most charming man imaginable? I
declare, I am half in love with him myself, and never
thought to find so perfect a match in every way for my
Livia. And as you see, not a bit puffed up, or forever
looking down his nose at those less exalted than he is, as
some I could mention. So handsome! So exactly the gentleman!"

She sighed rapturously, and it was obvious that nothing else, not even her niece's near tragedy, could compete at the moment with her present sense of triumph.

"He is certainly very—charming," answered Sorrel
truthfully if reluctantly. "But not at all what I had expected. And you didn't tell me Mr. FitzSimmons was invited as well."

"Didn't I? I declare it is scarcely any wonder, for I
scarce know what I am about lately with all the excitement and—but never mind that!" she interrupted herself

hastily. "Until Lord Wycherly came upon the scene he was the most prominent aspirant for Livia's hand, you know. It is a shame he has no title, but he is related to half the noble houses of England, and is very fashionable. At one point I believed they would make a match of it, for although he has scarcely a penny to bless himself with, that little matters after all, for the Lord knows I am wealthy enough to afford him. But that is neither here nor there now of course, for Livy has no eyes for anyone but this precious marquis, and I'm sure I don't blame her. Even without a title he would be exactly what I would wish for her."

"But why invite Mr. FitzSimmons at such a time?" persisted Sorrel. "Surely he will only be in the way?"

"Oh, well, that was Livy's doing," confided her aunt. "It appears they are good friends—they went to school together or some such—and I am sure it was only natural to invite them both. And it will make the numbers even, for despite your still being in black gloves, my love, I am determined that you shall not mope about as you did in London and refuse to appear in public."

Sorrel did not believe for one minute that her cousin was at all concerned about supplying an escort for her—unless, of course, it was to leave a clear field for herself with the marquis. More than likely she meant to play them off against each other, which sounded more like her. But in any case, she might leave Sorrel herself out of her machinations.

But before she could say so, her aunt went on, quite happily unaware that her niece did not share her own enthusiasm on the subject. "But, oh, my love! Only to think of Livy becoming a marchioness, which is something I never thought to see, despite her beauty! I can scarce contain my glee, for you must know there were many who predicted she would never succeed in catching a title for herself, despite all my blunt. And won't they look blue when the engagement is announced!"

She dwelled on this beatific vision for a few seconds,

then abruptly became more practical. "But that is not what I came to talk of, after all. You still look alarmingly pale. Should you not be laid down upon your bed, my dear? His lordship said you took a blow to the head and were knocked quite unconscious, and I can see you are still looking scarcely yourself. Dearest, I don't mean to scold, especially at such a moment, but whatever your father may allow—and from everything I've ever heard, I can't imagine what he can be thinking of, for I'm sure America must be a most dangerous place—but anyway, I cannot approve of these solitary rides of yours. And now you see what can become of them. I should never forgive myself if something happened to you while you were here."

Sorrel felt ridiculously guilty in the face of so much kindness, and said hastily, "Dearest Aunt Lela, I am only sorry to have distressed you. And that I risked Walter's chestnut. I only hope it may not be permanently lamed."

But her aunt easily dismissed her husband's claims to be upset in the matter. "Lord, dear, that's the least of my worries," she said frankly. "When I first saw you, looking so pale and shaken, I feared—but never mind that," she said hastily again. "And as for Walter, if I don't mind, I am sure he has no reason to. It's my money that paid for the chestnut, after all—and everything else, when all's said and done. If that were the only consideration, I'm sure you'd be welcome to ride any of his horses you choose. Not that it don't serve him right even if the chestnut is lamed, and I can tell you I'm saving up a few home truths to say to that husband of mine, if and when he condescends to return. Which I must admit I hope and pray he won't do any time soon, for I've no wish for him to be here during the marquis's visit, putting his oar in and very likely ruining everything. For whatever he may wish me to believe, and for all his birth, which he is forever boasting of, you won't convince me that he's any more welcome to the *ton* than what I am. And to have him here, no doubt making up to his lordship and pretending that he is on the best of terms with him, and very likely giving the marquis a disgust of all of us, would just be the last straw. Though ten to one he's getting up to more mischief which it will be my doubtful pleasure to rescue him from. I only wish I had known then what I know now! I hope I'm not one to boast, but it's unlike me to be sold a Smithfield bargain, and what I thought I wanted with another husband, when I'd buried two, is more than I can tell you. Not that I mean I'm tight with my blunt, as I hope you know, my love. But when it comes to paying five thousand pounds all to settle his gambling debts, when I give him an extremely generous allowance already, it's the outside of enough, and so I mean to tell him. Well, I told him it was the last time, but I doubt he believes me. He knows very well that I'd pay a good sight more than that to keep from having my Livy's chances spoiled by him creating a scandal! Which no doubt is exactly what he is counting on," she added bitterly.

Sorrel had to bite back a smile, despite her aching head, for her aunt's frankness on the subject of her third marriage had been a source of amusement to her from the beginning. No more than her aunt did she believe Mr. Walter Granville either able to live within his extremely generous allowance, or believe that his wife would not pay up if scandal threatened again. He was some years younger than her aunt, and as he never tired of throwing up to her, much better born. Sorrel's democratic principles had also been affronted that he could make her usually sensible aunt, who was still attractive and certainly held the purse strings, feel inferior merely because of her birth, but so it was. She had always been amazed at the inadequacies people put themselves through.

But she had to admit she herself did not like her aunt's third husband. Though amusing when he chose to be and not bad-looking, he was quite as vain and selfish as his step-daughter, with whom he did not get along. His interpretation of the married state seemed to be that it was his wife's duty to bail him out of trouble and supply his expensive wants, while he remained free to be odiously superior on the subject of the source of her wealth, and her humble beginnings, whenever he himself was out of sorts or she had been making him feel her hand on the reins too tightly.

"Not," added her aunt with unwonted gloominess, after thinking it over for a moment, "that for all I have been looking forward to this day, I almost wish his lordship had not come, for if it should go wrong, and through me, Livia would never forgive me."

"Why, Aunt," said Sorrel, startled by this unexpected turn. "How could it go wrong? And even if it did, it would scarcely be your fault, surely?"

Aunt Lela hesitated, then seemed to come to some conclusion, for she lowered her voice and glanced toward the closed door as if she feared even the walls had ears. "Well, I hadn't meant to tell you, my dear, for it's not your concern, and I didn't wish to worry you. But I must confess that when I saw you ride up, so pale and ill-looking, it gave me a regular turn, I can tell you! Are you sure it was no more than an accident, my love?" she insisted unexpectedly.

Sorrel was frowning in surprise. "Of course it was. The saddle slipped and I took a—" She broke off, for one fatal moment herself unsure. Then she shook off the nonsensical thought. "Aunt, you must tell me what has happened," she added more strongly.

"I'm sure I scarcely know whether I am on my head or my heels, my love. If you must know, I received a most—most unpleasant letter today, and as I say, when I saw you hurt, I feared—dearest, you must promise me you won't ride out alone anymore. It is far too dangerous!"

Sorrel was by then wholly mystified. "Why on earth should it be dangerous? What did the letter say, ma'am? Who was it from?"

"As to who it was from, I am sure I don't know," said her aunt indignantly. "But it threatened harm to either you or Livia unless I pay a great deal of money. So you see why I could not help but wonder if your accident might have been no accident after all, but a deliberate attempt to harm you in order to make me pay up."

Chapter 5

Sorrel could only gape at her aunt. "Good God, ma'am! Why, that's blackmail! How much did the letter demand?"

"Ten thousand pounds," said her aunt bitterly. "You can see why, when I saw you returning on Lord Wycherly's saddlebow so soon after receiving it, I naturally feared——but if you did no more than take a toss, I'm sure I don't know what to think!"

Sorrel's brain was suddenly busy again with unwelcome thoughts, for at the time she had wondered how the girth could have loosened so abruptly, without her being aware of it earlier. But she thought it best not to share her sudden suspicions with her aunt, and so said instead, "Dearest ma'am, I hope you do not mean to give in to such demands?"

"That's all very well for you to say, my love, and I confess I've no liking for being bled. It's the wickedness of it that has me the most upset. But I hope it goes without saying that I would far rather pay any amount than risk danger coming to either you or Livia. And you must admit it could not have happened at a worse moment—not that I mean to suggest there could be a good moment for such a thing—for there's Lord Wycherly to be considered. And allow this to spoil my Livy's chances I will not, however much I may dislike being swindled."

"Lord Wycherly? Why, what has he to say to anything?" asked Sorrel, honestly mystified.

Her aunt stared at her in astonishment. "Goodness

gracious, girl, I declare you are as distracted as I am—or else you did indeed addle your brains when you hit your head. He has everything to say to it, especially now, of all times. I would pay twice the sum demanded to keep from upsetting things just at this delicate juncture, for if he should hedge off because of it, I would never forgive myself. Nor would Livy, which is even more to the point," she added unanswerably.

Sorrel still had no wish to discuss the marquis, but she said slowly, against her will, "Are you indeed so sure that Lord Wycherly means to offer for Livia, dearest Aunt?"

"Bless you, love, why else would he have accepted my invitation? Why, anyone can tell he's nutty on her—not that there's anything new in that. They all are, and you'd be surprised at the number of men who are old enough to know better who make complete fools of themselves over her. It puts me in mind of when your mother and me was first out. Lord, the heads we turned then!" She sighed gustily, as if for times gone by, but then shook her head and returned to matters of more moment. "But he means to come up to scratch all right, which is why nothing must happen to mar the visit in any way. For there's no use blinking the fact that he's marrying beneath him in the eyes of the world, despite Livy's beauty and my money. You may be equally sure that he would hedge off without hesitation were he to get wind of even a whiff of scandal touching her. And that I won't let happen, if it costs me every penny I've got."

Sorrel could not see what the one had to do with the other, but she had long since given up trying to understand the delicate negotiations that seemed to be required in an English courtship. Nor, remembering her own recent conduct, did she feel she had much room to criticize. Indeed, she hoped for her aunt's sake, that the marquis would not hedge off for quite a different reason after her disclosures of the morning. But she said merely, and even more unwillingly, "But surely, ma'am, if he's the man you think him, he would not be deterred by something that's in no way your fault. And it is certainly not Livia's.''

"Well, that's where you're wrong, my dear," said her aunt shrewdly. "And no wonder, for you've little understanding of the snobbery that goes on here. You don't need to hide from me that you think Livy's shallow to have set her sights so on a title, for all you're too kind to say so," she added, to her niece's acute embarrassment. "In fact, I sometimes wonder if your mother weren't smarter to go to America, where things seem to me to be more open. Why, you wouldn't countenance the number of snubs that have been dealt me over the years, merely because my money derives from trade, and because I can't trace my ancestry all the way back to the Conqueror! And between you and me, my love, though I wouldn't dare say it to anyone else, that has always seemed the most absurd of things to base your pride upon! As though there didn't have to be the usual number of scaff and raff in the Conqueror's tail as anywhere else, and why that is considered such a thing to boast of is more than I can tell you.''

Despite everything, Sorrel could not help laughing at that. "Exactly so, ma'am. And surely, if Lord Wycherly is one of those, he is not the husband you would wish for Livia.''

"What I wish has very little to do with the matter, not when Livy has her heart set on him, which I fear she does," retorted her aunt even more unanswerably. "But that is neither here nor there. And the last laugh is mine, after all, for I can buy and sell the most of those who are too starched up to give me so much as a common bow in passing. And that is why I will not have his lordship upset by all this. In fact, you must promise me, my love, that you won't tell him!''

Her aunt looked so very alarmed at the prospect, that Sorrel reluctantly promised her. Besides, under the circumstances she did not anticipate making a bosom bow of the noble marquis. She would be happy never to have to speak to him again.

Besides, she could see that her aunt desired the match almost as much as her daughter did, perhaps to pay back all those people who had dared to snub her over the years. "That is all very well, ma'am," she said at last. "But it seems to me that if you are being blackmailed, the only thing to do is to lay it before the proper authorities."

But Aunt Lela was almost as alarmed by that sensible suggestion. "Report it?" she cried in the liveliest horror. "Are you *mad*? Yes, I can just see me reporting it and having a Bow Street Runner ensconced on the premises, as like as not, just at the moment we've his lordship in the house. Haven't I just been telling you that I won't have anything upsetting him, just as he's all set to pop the question at any moment?"

"But, dearest ma'am, you can't just give in to such blackmail," protested Sorrel. "Don't you know that will scarcely be the end of it? If you once pay up, it will go on and on, and I doubt even your fortune is big enough to stand that."

"Oh, well," said her aunt, ever practical. "Of course I don't intend to allow myself to be bled forever. Just until things are settled between Livy and the marquis. Besides, it may all turn out to be no more than a hoax, anyway, which I'm sure I hope it may. It was just learning of your accident, and wondering if it mightn't have been more than an accident, that made me blurt it out as I did. For as I said, I would never forgive myself if something should happen to you while you were under my roof."

Sorrel impulsively hugged her, and her aunt patted her hand and said more prosaically, "Not that it is my roof, of course, for I've only hired it for the season. And you may be sure I shall give that wretched Mr. Clemson a piece of my mind when next I write to him, for he assured me that everything was as it should be, and the staff most reliable. Now I have had to grease that odious

Mrs. Dowling in the fist to get her to stay, for of course
she knows she has me over a barrel, and did not hesitate
to use the fact! Odious creature! Not that I begrudge the
expense, as I hope you know. But it is the principle of
the thing. I wouldn't wonder at it if she put her wretched
niece up to the whole thing in the first place."

Sorrel was at least glad of the change of topic. "Dearest Aunt Lela, I, too, would put little past her. But I do
not think the maid in question had the wits to—er—deliberately provoke my cousin."

Her aunt took this implied criticism in good part. "No,
and however partial some people may think I am, I hope
I am not blind to my daughter's faults. In fact I have
scolded her quite sharply, for if Mrs. Dowling were to
take a pet and walk out, I daresay it would take weeks to
get someone from London to take her place, and then
where should we be? Not that I mean she should have
slapped the wretched girl, for if there is one thing more
than another that men dislike, it is the vulgar pulling of
caps, and so I have been at pains to inform her. When
she is my lady marchioness, she may afford to lose her
temper, but not before if she knows what's good for her.
But there, forgive me, my dear. I am chattering on like a
fiddlestick, when I daresay your head is aching something chronic. In fact, you should be laid down upon
your bed, and that is what I came up to see to, not to
bother you with my nonsense."

"No, no, my head doesn't ache—or only a very little.
But if you won't report it to the proper authorities, I
can't help but think the best thing you could do is go to
my lord Wycherly with your problem, ma'am," said Sorrel even more reluctantly. "He—didn't strike me as the
type who would be dismayed by much of anything. And
you may depend upon it he would know how to deal
with such a thing far better than either of us do."

But her aunt showed signs of fresh alarm at that. "My
love, have I not been telling you that I won't have anything threaten this visit? One breath of scandal and he

will shear off and that will be the end of it. And you are not to tell him either! You gave me your word, remember!"

When Sorrel reluctantly reaffirmed her promise, her aunt relaxed again. "It would be different, of course, if he were merely marrying Livia for my money. In fact, I almost wish that he were."

Sorrel was resigned to a great deal, but that was too much. "You would *prefer* that he wished to marry Livia only for her money, ma'am?" she repeated incredulously.

"No, of course not. Though heaven knows I can stand the nonsense, and at least then I would know where I was with him. Pound dealing is something I do understand, and I would be more sure of him if I knew I had a hold over him. More, I would be in a position to see he treated her right after the wedding, for you may be sure I would not hand over the dibs all at once! You've no notion, my dear, and I'm thankful you don't, of how little one knows about a man until you're married to him, however charming he may appear on the surface. I should know, for I've had three husbands myself, and the more fool me for marrying the third one. But that's neither here nor there, except that you may be sure the last thing I will do is call in a Bow Street Runner, my love, or let his lordship learn anything of what is threatened. I tell you I would pay such a paltry amount a dozen times before I would do that. Nor I can't risk either of you two girls being hurt. I shall just have to pay the dratted sum and resign myself to it, at least until Livy is safely wed."

Sorrel privately thought the news would come decidedly worse after the wedding, if her aunt feared his lordship's reaction to it so much. But by then, of course, he would be in little position to object, which was clearly her aunt's purpose.

She also thought her cousin a far more likely target than herself, if the intent was to frighten her aunt into paying over such a large sum of money. But she had no intention of saying that either and frightening her aunt still further. Instead she asked curiously, "How was the money to be paid, ma'am?"

"That I don't know yet. He was to give me further instructions. Stringing me along, more like, merely to make me more anxious!" she said resentfully.

"You say 'he.' Do you know for a fact that it's a man?"

"No, but who else could it be? Not that it matters who it is. They shall have to be paid, though it goes against the grain."

"At least don't give in yet, ma'am," Sorrel begged her. "I have an idea or two in my head. Besides, perhaps it is no more than a hoax, as you said."

"Well, I am sure I hope it may be," said her aunt frankly, rising to her feet again and shaking out her crumpled skirts. "At least I'm bound to say you've got some color back now, and have been talking sensibly, which is something to be grateful for. I hope you know, my dear, that I would pay a great deal more than ten thousand pounds to protect you while you are in my care, and if I thought for a moment that your fall was in any way my fault, I would never forgive myself."

Sorrel rose in turn and kissed her aunt with real affection. "No, no, Aunt Lela, whatever may be the truth of the rest, I am convinced it was merely due to my own folly, not some nefarious plot against me," she assured her soothingly, if not wholly truthfully. "Which reminds me. Have you told my cousin of the letter?"

"No, and I don't mean to," said her aunt decidedly. "I've no wish for her to be upset at such a time, and anyway, I daresay that between the pair of them, Lord Wycherly and Mr. FitzSimmons will be able to protect her well enough." She chuckled richly. "It's certain they'll be glued to her side for the coming fortnight. Besides, ten to one it's only someone's twisted idea of humor, and will all turn out to be no more than a hum.

But you be careful, my love. I don't wish to scold you, and it seems clear you're used to mighty different standards of conduct, but it seems to me you are at a great deal more risk than my Livia is, in jauntering about all over the place on your own."

"I'll be careful, dearest Auntie," Sorrel said confidently.

Chapter 6

Afterward Sorrel was to remember that misplaced confidence with a certain amount of irony.

But for the present, she used her headache as an excuse not to go down to dinner that evening, having no wish to be obliged to confront his lordship again so soon. Instead she had an early night, for she had a good deal to think about, little of it pleasant.

Whether because of that, or because it was impossible to find a comfortable place to lay her bruised head, she tossed and turned restlessly most of the night, and woke unrefreshed, with nothing resolved except that she did not look forward to the next week or so.

The bump on her head was still tender enough to make it painful to brush her hair, and the vestige of a headache lingered behind her eyes, but at least she had not—as she had half-feared—developed a black eye during the night to add to her miseries. Then she caught herself up in some annoyance, knowing that next to her beautiful cousin she might have two black eyes and a broken nose and no one would notice. She dressed with some slowness, finding herself sore in places she had not suspected, and went reluctantly downstairs.

Though she had been troubled by some lurid dreams during the night, in the clear light of morning she was inclined to dismiss her aunt's startling disclosure. Her accident certainly could have been engineered, but she still thought any attempt to frighten her aunt into disgorging large sums would be aimed toward her cousin, not herself. Besides, in all probability it was indeed nothing but a rather cruel hoax.

Unfortunately, her other most immediate problem was not so easy of solution. She had made a complete fool of herself in front of the marquis yesterday, and if she was inclined to be angry all over again whenever she thought of the unpleasant jest he had played upon her, there was no denying that her own indiscreet tongue was a good deal to blame. She cringed whenever she remembered some of the things she had said, and though in the ordinary course of events she would merely have shrugged it off, she knew that if the marquis were to take offense and refuse to offer for her cousin because of it, she did not know how she would ever look her aunt in the face again.

Since he had deliberately invited her unflattering opinion of him, she did not see how he could have the gall to take offense. But she made no claim to familiarity with the English aristocracy. Everything he had told her had patently been a lie, which only made her despise him all the more. It obviously had amused him and the supercilious Mr. FitzSimmons to encourage her to make a fool of herself, and she did not doubt they had laughed heartily later at her ignorance and her bumptious opinions.

None of which was designed to put her in sympathy with the odious marquis. Though, if the truth be admitted, she was still having some trouble reconciling her picture of the starched-up nobleman with the quiet, confident man on horseback whom she had liked so very much. And if she could not help but frown a little over his sympathy and his charming smile, when she should instead be remembering how he had tricked and humiliated her, then the more fool she.

She certainly meant to put off the moment they came face-to-face for as long as possible. And since she knew her cousin's habit of rising late, and did not expect either of the guests to be up at so early an hour either, she took the opportunity to go down to the stables to check on the chestnut.

It was the time of day she had always liked best, and the cool English morning was very different from what she was used to. She found the chestnut still favoring his off fore, but could find no trace of a scrape or any swelling. With relief she gave him a carrot and patted him, and was just turning away when she heard a step behind her.

She glanced up, thinking it would be her aunt's groom. But unexpectedly it was the marquis making his way toward her.

Her heart jumped, to her extreme annoyance, but she determinedly straightened her shoulders and her spine and turned to greet him, seeing with resentment that he looked even more handsome that morning, in a coat of blue superfine that exactly matched his eyes. Despite her anger, for her aunt's sake, she could not afford to tell him exactly what she thought of him. "My lord," she said stiffly.

His lips seemed to twitch, but he said as formally, "Miss Kent. How is the chestnut? I looked him over yesterday afternoon and could discover no lasting injury. I believe he will soon be as good as new."

She drew a deep breath, refusing to be drawn into an ordinary pleasant exchange. "Thank you. My lord—"

He went on as if she had not spoken. "I am delighted to see you, but should you be up? Forgive me for saying so, but you still look a little pale, and you did not come down to dinner last night."

It was on the tip of her tongue to tell him exactly why, but again she determinedly controlled it. "I am perfectly well today, thank you!" She said coldly. "I told you I was unlikely to be overcome by a mere toss." She determinedly tried again. "My lord—"

"Miss Kent—" he said at the same time.

Both halted, and he laughed, though she did not. But she took advantage of the brief confusion to say stonily.

"I wish to apologize to you for the things I said yesterday."

He closed the door of the stall for her and began to walk with her back toward the house, as if theirs was the most normal of friendly meetings. Once more in his presence she had to reluctantly acknowledge a powerful charm that was almost palpable. And despite everything he had most understanding eyes. "Which ones?" he asked curiously. "That you dislike the aristocracy, or had clearly determined to despise me even before I came?"

It was apparent he was not going to make it easy for her. She gritted her teeth. "Whatever may be—my private thoughts, I should not have blurted them out to a chance-met stranger. I apologize for that. I can only claim a—a bump on the head as my excuse, and beg you to forget it."

His eyes danced a little, but he murmured with deliberate provocation. "Oh, craven, Miss Kent! I am disappointed in you. Besides, I have a most inconvenient memory, I'm afraid. Do you wish me to believe you didn't mean the things you said about my rank and position?"

This was too much. She said angrily, "On the contrary, I meant everything I said! I apologize merely for having said it to your face."

He burst out laughing. "Ah, worse and worse! No, don't poker up! I am done teasing you. I am perfectly aware that it is I who should be begging your pardon, Miss Kent. Are you very angry with me? I acknowledge that it was unforgivable, but I couldn't resist. It is a long time since I have met with such a sweeping rebuff. In general, you know, I meet with too much exaggerated respect for a title that you quite rightly pointed out I did nothing to earn. In fact, you can't know how refreshing it was to hear my rank thrown into my teeth, and all my pretensions so summarily dealt with."

This was so ingenuous as to be wholly unbelievable. Did he really believe her such a fool, or so easily to be taken in by a charming smile? But since she did not relish the probable answer to either question, she remained silent.

"Come now," he said in amusement. "Fair is fair. If there is an ounce of truth in you, you will at least admit that for all my faults I am not—how did it go?—deaf, blind, or halt in one leg, so I can't be quite as bad as you were expecting."

Abruptly he held out his hand and smiled down at her coaxingly, "Let us cry a truce! Is what I did so very unforgivable?"

She was honest enough—at least with herself—to know that ordinarily it would not have been. It was merely the humiliating circumstances—and her own instinctive liking for him—that made her so hurt and angry now. But she was not about to admit as much to him. "I have no doubt it amused you very much to make a fool of me. But did you have to lie to do it?"

He frowned swiftly. "I did not lie to you. Or if I did, it was only by omission, I assure you. I confess I should have revealed who I was sooner. But I was enjoying your unconventional views too much, to wish to put an end to your confidences. Confess, you would not have revealed half so much if you had known who I was."

"It was more than by omission," she said coldly. "Or did you not claim to have been a soldier? You obviously guessed it was the one thing that would impress me."

The amusement had completely disappeared from his eyes. "Ah, if you thought that, you indeed have every reason to be angry with me," he said ruefully. "But I wasn't lying. Until very recently I was no more than a captain in the Rifles. Didn't your aunt tell you?"

She lifted her eyes to his face, no longer knowing what to believe. "No, she didn't," she conceded unwillingly after a moment.

He smiled at her again. "Well, it's true. I spent most of the last ten years in the Peninsula, and sold out only two years ago, when I came into the title. And that must serve as my excuse, I suppose. If you must know, for a little while you allowed me to pretend that I was still a soldier, and not a marquis, and for that I was grateful to you. Please believe that I never meant to hurt your feelings, or belittle you in any way."

He looked so sincere that she was again thrown off balance, and that annoyed her even more. They had reached the terrace by then, and she said with an incredulous smile, "I think you must indeed believe me a fool, my lord. Do you seriously expect me to believe you don't *like* being a marquis?"

"Is it so impossible to believe?" he demanded coolly. "My title has its uses, I will be the first to admit. Let us rather say, I liked being a plain soldier even better. You were exactly right, you know, Miss Kent, in your contempt for the aristocracy. It is appalling how differently a marquis is treated, and how difficult it is to find anyone who will stand up to you, or speak the truth. Usually new acquaintances—especially young and unmarried females or their mamas—are all too aware of my rank. But you showed me you didn't care a fig for my vaunted importance, and I liked you for it."

But that had prompted a new and even more unwelcome suspicion. "Especially unmarried females!" she repeated. "*Now* I begin to understand your extraordinary behavior of yesterday. You suspected me of having deliberately set out to waylay you, and of staging the whole accident, just to gain your attention. Didn't you?"

When he said nothing, she added more hotly, "I see you do not deny it! You may still believe it to be true, in fact."

"Oh, my unruly tongue! I suppose I deserve it, for I should have known you would latch on to the most unflattering interpretation possible. Miss Kent, there is no way I can either deny or refute your charges, without sounding even more of a coxcomb than I must already," he said ruefully. "Suffice it to say that if I ever cherished any such unworthy suspicions about you, they were soon laid to rest. Besides, there could be no mistaking the genuineness of your accident. In fact, you still do not look as strong as you would have me believe."

She brushed that aside. "That is hardly proof. I suppose I might have thought the advantages worth the risk. Or miscalculated and suffered more hurt than I intended," she countered bitterly. "But then I daresay you are accustomed to having women throwing themselves at you in the most unlikeliest of ways, and so could not help but be suspicious."

He did not attempt to deny that either, but said instead, teasingly, "Rest assured, ma'am, that if the genuineness of your faint had not already convinced me, the unorthodoxy of your democratic principles soon would have. In fact, it was amusing to have my noble pretensions reduced to such uncompromising truths, for once. I therefore acquit you of having any intention of setting your cap at me to acquire my title—and what a vulgar phrase that is. You will indeed think I am a conceited coxcomb. But not conceited enough, I assure you, not to realize that as plain Captain Langford I was regarded as no very great prize. It is my title, not myself, that is so much sought-after, as you so correctly surmised."

She still did not know what to believe and what not. Certainly, if he felt like that, she could not imagine what he was doing with her beautiful cousin Livia. On the other hand, it seemed difficult to credit that so handsome and assured a man could believe himself sought after merely because of his title. She was used to thinking those sorts of foolish inadequacies were strictly her own.

"What I think," she said even more bitterly, "is that you are an admirable tactician, my lord. In fact, the one thing I do believe among that farrago of lies you told me yesterday is that you were a soldier. But if you indeed still harbor any doubts that I am the sort of contemptible, ambitious female to scheme to marry a title, and be willing to cut out my own cousin in the bargain, you did not mention the one consideration that must surely have convinced you of the truth more than any other."

He looked again annoyingly amused. "I hesitate to ask, but what is that, Miss Kent?"

"That I stand about as much chance of cutting out my extremely beautiful cousin as you do of convincing me you yourself harbor secret democratic principles—my lord!"

The ready laughter sprang to his eyes, but he said gravely, "And yet, even stranger things have happened—on both counts."

"Yes. That I could expect you to ever tell me the truth, for one!" she countered swiftly.

"At least I am slightly encouraged, for I feared I had permanently silenced your outspoken tongue. But you needn't keep slapping me down, Miss Kent. I have already apologized most abjectly."

She almost gasped. "Well, if you consider it an abject apology to throw up my foolish words to me at every opportunity, I do not!"

He laughed. "No, no. That would be most unhandsome. Almost as unhandsome as judging someone on a mere circumstance of birth. Don't you agree, Miss Kent?"

She had to wrestle most strongly with herself not to laugh. "Now we see the value of your apology. I must warn you, my lord, that you are fast hardening into conviction what was, I'll admit, no more than a foolish prejudice on my part. First you deliberately led me to make a fool of myself, and then refuse to let me forget what was uttered out of a blow on the head and, I make no doubt, the brandy you deliberately poured down my throat. I can only hope, if there is any decency in *you* at all—which I am beginning to doubt—that you will at least refrain from betraying me to my aunt and my cousin."

He burst out laughing. "And now we discover the value of your apology as well. You clearly care little about having offended me, and merely fear being exposed to your aunt and cousin. No, no! I have done with teasing you. I will own that I am indeed to blame for provoking you so shamelessly. As I said before, let us cry a truce."

She still regarded him a little suspiciously, but at last put her hand unwillingly in the one he again held out to her. But she could not resist murmuring with deliberate provocation, "But then, I have little doubt you consider that your rank entitles you to such license, my lord."

His mobile mouth acknowledged the hit, but he said promptly, "Not in the least, Miss Kent. And if ever I do fall into that trap, I will count on you to remind me of the error in my ways."

"But then, I am only here for a few more months, my lord," she said even more dulcetly.

He grinned again. "Meaning that it is a full-time occupation? I begin to think you will indeed be good for me, Miss Kent." Unexpectedly he raised the hand he still held and lightly kissed it before releasing it again.

She almost snatched it back and turned quickly to hide the sudden color in her face. Despite everything the tug of liking between them was still strong, and she had need to be wary. Almost at random she demanded. "Do you really have women throwing themselves at you—all for the sake of your title?"

"By the dozens!" he answered promptly. "I can scarce stir a step without having to remove them from my path. Modesty naturally forbids my revealing to you the extent of the problem, but I have had young ladies envious of becoming a marchioness sprain their ankles when I am around to catch them, lose control of their mounts when galloping on Rotten Row when I am there to rescue them, and stage carriage accidents before my door. I give you my word I seldom know a moment's peace. In fact, it is remarkable how attractive I became once I had gained a title."

He spoke lightly, but his very lightness made her suspect there was more truth to his words than he would have her believe. More and more she wondered what he was doing mixed up with her beautiful cousin. But she said dryly, "At least you may retire me from the lists, my lord. I assure you I don't aspire to a title. I can only wonder that you don't renounce it yourself, if it is that much of a nuisance."

"Ah, I can tell you still don't believe me, Miss Kent. But the decision was a harder one than you might know. It is all my uncle's fault for having been so foolish as to have died childless. Since that time, I have had ample opportunity to learn how a title has changed the way I am regarded in the eyes of the world. Believe me, you can have no more jaded a view of the nobility than I do at this point. People I had scarcely exchanged a common bow with are now my bosom bows, and matchmaking mamas who considered me previously to have been but a negligible prospect are now inviting me to run tame about their houses. As for the flattering attention—not to say toad eating—I get from such inferior personages as tailors, landlords, and ivory-turners—in short, anyone who hopes to sell me anything or cheat me out of something—why, I could be forgiven for getting so insufferably above myself. Or at least I could, did I not remember the very different treatment I was meted out before my sudden ascension to my present status."

She was frowning a little, for she had to admit she had never before considered it in that light. But after a moment said with some irony, "Why thank you, my lord. You have cured me, as nothing else ever has, of looking only at the surface of things. It sounds horrid."

"No, no, it is not as bad as that. Why, what an ungrateful fellow I must sound. You must know, Miss Kent, that were I to utter such heresy to any but yourself, they would quite rightly consider that I had taken leave of my senses. And sometimes I suspect I have. How can I explain it? I do not, I confess, ascribe to your democratic principles completely, but I have spent the better part of my life being judged on my own merits, and I liked it. Certainly I found that being obliged to give it up for the sake of a title I'd no wish for in the first place was among the hardest of the adjustments I had to make."

She still did not know how much to believe him. It seemed clear he knew how to make himself agreeable to women, and he must know exactly what was designed to please her. But she could not quite believe it was all assumed for her benefit. "But surely you must have known that you were your uncle's heir?"

"Knowing that I would someday step into his shoes, and being obliged to do so are two different things, however." He shrugged, "I am well aware that I am generally regarded as a lucky devil, rather to be envied than pitied. And so I daresay I am. I am everywhere kowtowed to, as you pointed out, and sought after and toad eaten. I daresay it is most odd in me—not to mention deuced ungrateful—to have found it preferable to be mere Captain Langford, as I said."

"Forgive me. I understand these things very little. But if you sincerely feel that way, is there no way you could have avoided it?"

His rueful grin reappeared. "Unfortunately, I have been reared to consider it an obligation and a duty, however much I might have wished my uncle had the forethought to provide himself with a dozen sons. Besides, I don't wish to present myself to you as owning a virtue that is undeserved. In fact my attitude is purely selfish! I merely wished to continue in a way of life I found very much to my taste. But I am sure you would be the first to agree we cannot always have what we want out of this life."

She was frowning slightly again. "No, that at least is true. But if you disliked being obliged to sell out so much, why did you? Surely no one could compel you to do that at least?"

"The position I inherited has duties as well as privileges attached to it. A great many people rely upon me for their living—a deuced sight too many, in fact! And then, too, there is the question of an heir. I could not square it with my conscience to continue a way of life that was, admittedly, preferable to me, merely for my own selfish enjoyment, when so much else depended upon me. And now perhaps you see, Miss Kent, why I am also grateful to you."

He had again surprised her. "To me? What reason on earth do you have to be grateful to me?" she demanded suspiciously.

"Because I believe you are the first person I have been able to say this to. Everyone else believes I must naturally have been elated at my good fortune, and it seemed churlish to point out the truth—that I'd as lief not have stepped into my uncle's shoes and his responsibilities— at least for some years yet! Even my army friends, though sad to see me go, were quietly happy for my good fortune. It is only you, with your prejudice against the false folly of titles, who is perhaps capable of hearing and understanding the truth."

She did not know what to say—or whether he was again making sport of her. Again it was on the tip of her unruly tongue to ask what he was doing, offering for her ambitious cousin if he felt that way. But she feared she had done quite enough damage already. "In that case I must be pleased to have been of service," she answered dryly at last.

He smiled at her and said even more unexpectedly, "And none of this is what I wished to talk to you about. I can't think how I came to bore on and on about my troubles. You must be a remarkably sympathetic listener, Miss Kent."

She felt bound to point out truthfully, "On the contrary, I fear I have not been in the least sympathetic."

He laughed. "No, but then it would seem that was what I needed, little though I realized it. I must confess you have an unexpected way of looking at things that I find most refreshing. But that, too, is not in the least what I wished to talk to you about."

She was frowning again. "You had a reason for seeking me out this morning, other than to apologize to me? An apology, I must point out, that was wholly insincere. If so, I can't imagine what it was."

He again looked amused, but only briefly. She discovered, somewhat to her surprise, that his handsome face could look surprisingly serious—even a little grim.

"We are getting along so excellently, despite our unfortunate beginning, that I hesitate to spoil things. But I have some—unfortunate news for you, I'm afraid."

She could only stare at him in bewilderment. "For me? What kind of unfortunate news?"

He sighed. "There is no easy way to say this. Who, Miss Kent, could have reason to wish to harm or even kill you? For that is what almost happened yesterday, I'm afraid."

Chapter 7

Sorrel was taken wholly off guard. "Wh—*what* did you say?"

"Who has a big enough grudge against you to wish to cause you harm—or even death?" Again he sounded unexpectedly grim. "For I'm afraid to say your fall yesterday was no accident."

But she had herself slightly better in hand by then, and said instantly, "No one. You are being absurd, my lord!"

"Am I? I only wish I were. I was curious and a little puzzled yesterday, especially after your horse managed to rid himself of his saddle completely. For while girths may break, certainly, surely a careful groom would spot so dangerous a defect, and it was obvious you yourself had noticed nothing amiss. So I had a talk with your aunt's groom—a most sound fellow, by the way. He certainly disapproves of your riding out alone, but I acquit him of carelessness. And he admitted grudgingly that you possess a most excellent seat and nice, light hands—which I can attest to myself. He furthermore assured me that the saddle you used was all but new, for apparently your aunt is most particular about how things are kept, and does not—er—object to laying out her blunt to good purpose. He himself was highly perturbed when the chestnut returned without his saddle, and was almost as puzzled as I was how it could have happened."

She could only stare at him breathlessly, knowing what was coming. "To make a long story short, Miss Kent, I was disturbed enough to send my own groom out to search for your lost saddle. He found it without too much difficulty, and his opinion on the subject nearly parallels my own—if not quite as profanely. Someone deliberately cut through your girth just enough that any unexpected pressure—such as a jump over a wall, which you are known to be prone to do—would cause it to break. It was done most cleverly, so that no one would notice, but it was done. In other words, Miss Kent, someone deliberately arranged your accident, and I would very much like to know who."

She was aghast at the information he had just given her, but it was no time to be considering that. If it was true, it could only be connected with the threat against her aunt, and the implications of that were too great to be taken in at the moment. But if so, the marquis was the last person her aunt wished to know about it. Indeed, she had given her promise she would not tell him.

"There must be some mistake," she said weakly. "No one could have any reason for wishing me any harm."

"The evidence would seem to indicate otherwise. Which leads me back to my original question, Miss Kent. Who finds you dangerous enough or a great enough threat to wish you dead?"

"No one," she repeated more strongly. "The whole thing is absurd."

She feared he did not believe her, but she had never been more glad to see her cousin in her life, for Livia strolled out at that moment, looking lovely in a sprig muslin with trailing ribbons and a charming chip-straw hat. She frowned a little at the sight of them together, but said merely, "Oh, there you are, my lord! Talking secrets?"

Sorrel feared she was blushing idiotically, but said quickly, before his lordship could intervene, "Not at all. Merely, Lord Wycherly was asking me what he might propose to entertain you, and I suggested a ride to the Broadway Tower my aunt has been telling us about." Her eyes dared him to refute her.

He did not, though he said warningly in a low voice, "Don't think you have heard the last of this from me, for you haven't, Miss Kent." He then raised his voice and said cheerfully. "Good morning, Miss Morden! I can tell by your bloom that you slept exceedingly well. Yes, your cousin has inspired me with an ambition to see this tower of yours. I hope we may make up an expedition while I'm here."

Livia looked again between the two of them in slight suspicion, but such was her vanity, as Sorrel knew well, that it was almost inconceivable to her that her mousy American cousin might be a potential rival. Her momentary jealousy sprang more from a general belief that all women were as ruthless as she was herself in pursuit of what she wanted, than any actual belief that something was going on between them.

So she tucked her hand intimately into her noble suitor's arm, and said gaily, "Oh, yes! Mama is forever prating of it, for evidently it was new-built when she was a girl, and it made a tremendous impression on her. I daresay it will turn out to be no great thing, but God knows there is little else to do. We can take a picnic and ride over one day."

She wholly ignored her cousin and began to walk with his lordship back toward the house. "But I was just come in search of you, for breakfast will be ready soon. Mr. FitzSimmons is yet to come down, but he assured me he is an even later riser than I am."

But Sorrel had already discovered for herself that the marquis had a mind of his own. He gently halted, forcing Livia to do the same, and looked back toward Sorrel with a question in his eyes—and something else that warned her he indeed did not mean to let her so lightly escape his questions. "But we are forgetting your cousin. Are you coming in to breakfast, Miss Kent?"

Sorrel was amused despite herself at her cousin's transparently annoyed expression, but she politely declined Wycherly's invitation. "No, I breakfasted hours ago."

"And sound odiously superior because of it," he countered. "Why is it, Miss Morden, that early risers are so generally contemptuous of the rest of us? And without any cause that I can see. Very well, we shall leave you then. But we must have a chat again soon, Miss Kent. Very soon," he added meaningfully, and allowed Livia to lead him into the house.

Sorrel was left to look after them with an odd grimace. She still did not know what to make of his unexpected revelations, but she had at least been right in one respect. It would be hard to find a couple more suited in looks, for both were golden creatures, sublimely well matched in terms of physical beauty. In fact, no one could help thinking, watching Livia cling so demurely to his arm, while he smiled attentively down at her, admiration openly to be read in his handsome countenance, that they were clearly meant for each other.

Then Sorrel was annoyed with herself for the stab that caused her, and determinedly turned her mind to far more important matters. If his lordship was right, then her fall had indeed been no accident, and that was disturbing enough. But if he was right, the last person her aunt wished to know of it was the marquis himself. And whatever else she might think of him, she knew enough by now to suspect that the noble Marquis of Wycherly was unlikely to be easily fobbed off with a few easy disclaimers.

As for her aunt, Sorrel didn't know whether to tell her the truth or not. Certainly it would only worry her, and incline her more than ever to pay the sum demanded; which was something Sorrel was determined to prevent if at all possible.

It was puzzling anyway. She was still convinced Livia, not herself, would be the more natural target if the intent was to blackmail her aunt. But then, perhaps Livia had been the intended victim after all. If the girth had indeed deliberately been made to break, it was admittedly more likely that she, and not her cousin, would be the one to be hurt, for Livia was known to be an indifferent horsewoman. But it was possible the blackmailer didn't know that.

Besides, whoever the intended victim had been, she was inclined to discount the marquis's assertion that the intent had been to seriously harm or even kill. In the normal course of events her own accident was unlikely to have produced anything but a painful fall and a few bruises. It was only by chance that she had hit her head on a stone and been hurt even as much as she was.

That was somewhat more comforting, for perhaps no real harm had been intended. The attempt had been meant merely to frighten her aunt into paying the demanded ransom.

If so, it would certainly succeed if her aunt knew of it, which inclined Sorrel not to tell her aunt yet awhile. It would be far preferable to try and discover the blackmailer for herself and expose him. For Sorrel, even more practical than her aunt, had no doubt that if Aunt Lela once gave in to such demands, she would never hear the last of it. Nor, American-bred and used to independence, did it occur to her to shirk such a task when confronted by it.

How to discover the blackmailer was the difficulty, of course. The attempt on the saddle made it look as if one of the servants might be involved. Those in the house, including the odious Mrs. Dowling, were local, and thus had very little loyalty to her aunt. But her aunt had brought her own coachman, butler, and French cook, as well as her groom and footman and both her own and Livia's expensive personal dressers from London with her.

Judging by the scene yesterday, the local servants might have reason for a grievance against her aunt—or more likely, against Livia. But would it manifest itself in

so farfetched a plot? She would not have said any of
them had the sophistication or the cunning to devise
such a plan. Besides, her aunt would be gone by the end
of the summer, and jobs were not that plentiful in the
country, surely, that anyone would be prepared to risk
theirs?

Unfortunately, it was equally impossible to tell about
her aunt's own servants, for Sorrel had known none of
them long enough. It might be someone either with a
grudge against her aunt, or merely with an eye to the future, which for the usual serving class could admittedly
be bleak enough. Again a grudge was certainly possible,
for Livia was demanding and scarcely concerned about
the sensibilities of the servants, and Sorrel knew there
was much grumbling belowstairs.

And yet there might be any number of others with reason to wish her aunt harm, or else wishful to make a
quick and illegal fortune. Sorrel had no way of knowing
what enemies her aunt might have made in the past, or
what jealous rivals of Livia's might exist. It might even
be someone from the village resentful over her aunt's
success. The possibilities, in fact, seemed endless.

Nor was it in the least comforting to realize—especially with her head still aching from yesterday—that if
the first attempt failed in its purpose, another might be
made. Again she wondered if her cousin should not be
warned.

But her promise to her aunt stood in her way there,
too. The only hopeful part of the whole business was
that if the marquis was right, her aunt would surely be
receiving a demand for money shortly, and then it might
be possible to lay some sort of a trap for the blackmailer.

But in the meantime, her most immediate worry might
well be how to keep the marquis from finding out any
more than he had already. Whatever else she thought of
him—and she was by no means certain what that was—
she was beginning to think him very far from a fool. On

many counts she would be as well to avoid any future tête-à-têtes with him.

Then she had to smile, for that was one area in which her cousin would do everything in her power to help her. And what Livia wanted, she usually managed to get.

The topic of the trip to the tower was still being discussed when Sorrel reluctantly joined the others for luncheon. Livia was at her gay and amusing best, making them laugh by her droll warnings of the dullness of the district and her own boredom until they came.

"For I promise you, even I was reduced to yawning over a book one afternoon. My cousin is almost a bluestocking, for I believe she was educated at some frightfully learned seminary or something, so it's all very well for her. But no one in London would have believed I could be reduced to such a pitiful state."

She looked up then and saw her cousin standing rigidly in the doorway, but showed no particular embarrassment at being overheard. "Oh, are you there, cousin?" she asked carelessly. "Well, I daresay it's nothing to be ashamed of."

"I am not in the least ashamed of it," said Sorrel quietly, and took her seat at the table as far away from the marquis as she could manage.

It was surprisingly Mr. FitzSimmons who rescued the slightly awkward situation. "At least you lie on one account, Miss Morden!" he said promptly. "I defy any place where you are to be in the least dull."

Livia gave her delicious gurgle of laughter. "Wait until you have spent a week here! And I haven't even told you the worse, though I suspect you have begun to discover it for yourselves after only one night spent here. I fear we got you here under false pretenses, for the house, which Mama hired for the summer, is not in the least comfortable and the servants are all untrained rustics. For all that my mother may have considered it the height of luxury when she was a girl, I can't think why people are always making over old houses. The rooms are all annoyingly cramped, and so dark and dreary that it makes me want to scream. Nor can one see out of the windows—not that there's anything much to see, I'll grant you that!—and the ceilings are so low I feel as if they are about to come down upon my head. I would have the whole thing pulled down and build a nice modern house in its stead."

Thus, thought Sorrel with irony, her cousin dispensed with a charming old Elizabethan house, with its mullioned windows and paneled rooms. She herself had fallen in love with it on sight, and found the intricately carved wainscoting within and the fanciful Elizabethan brick chimneys without extremely beautiful.

But it was again Mr. FitzSimmons who carried the conversation. "Then you need not worry, for Wycherly at least will feel right at home," he retorted. "You obviously have not seen *his* ancestral pile yet. Much grander than this, I promise you, and not a comfortable room in the house. Give you my word! I once spent a night or two there, and the fire in my bedchamber smoked, and there were ominous creakings all night long, which I took to be a mouse. But I was assured the next morning by the butler that it was nothing but the ghost of one of the earlier inhabitants who haunts the place. Fact! Just ask Wycherly!"

Livia looked to the marquis, half in amusement, half disbelief. "Oh, no! It can't be true! Is it?"

The marquis said with his misleading gravity. "Absolutely. We did not, of course, put him in one of the really haunted rooms, for no one dares to sleep there. As for comfort, when in residence there, I am required to wait half an hour after I ring for my shaving water to be brought to me, and by then it is usually cold, so great is the distance from the kitchens, and so long are the corridors. But that is doubtless a small enough price to pay for owning one of the country's stateliest homes. As for the chimneys, I have not discovered one that doesn't belch smoke," he added ruefully, "and I have grown inured to cold dinners and drafty halls. But then I was brought up in much more plebian comfort, I must admit."

"No, no, you are bamming me!" exclaimed Livia, laughing delightedly. "It is listed in all the guide books as a most distinguished residence. You are horrid, both of you. Besides, I do not mean really great houses, like Wycherly. But I confess I do like my comfort. In London I made Mama install one of the new water closets, and we spent a fortune rebuilding the chimneys so they wouldn't smoke. You cannot mean you are really uncomfortable there?"

The marquis smiled down at her in the heart-catching way he had, causing Livia to sparkle even more and Mr. FitzSimmons to glance at him rather jealously. "No— though this house seems snug by comparison. Besides, I am inured to discomfort after all my years on the Peninsula. *There* I was frequently glad merely to have a roof over my head and a mud floor beneath my blanket, and there were no chimneys at all, only a hole in the roof to let the smoke escape. I promise you this house looks positively luxurious by comparison. It is only Fitz here who is at all nice in his requirements, for by now I can sleep anywhere."

"Well," said Livia frankly, "I regard living here as almost as bad! As you discovered last night, we dine at so unfashionably early an hour that it is still light enough to require no candles, but I am assured that is what they mean by keeping country hours! But at least some evenings we may move the table out on the terrace and dine al fresco, and now that you are here, it will be charming. I make no doubt."

"But then your presence makes any place charming, Miss Morden," said Mr. FitzSimmons gallantly. "Isn't that so, Wycherly?"

The marquis had fallen into a slight abstraction for some reason, but he roused himself at that. "What? Oh, yes, indeed. But then you must know I am shockingly easy to please, and am very seldom bored."

Sorrel almost laughed, for this was less to Livia's liking. His lordship would have to watch it if he wished to curry favor with the spoiled beauty. But Livia went on to make elaborate plans for their entertainment while they were there. Aunt Lela was giving a dinner party that evening in honor of her distinguished guests, and had invited some old friends she had known since she was a girl, but Livia easily discounted that, having frankly informed her mother that his lordship was not in the least interested in a parcel of dowdies. She had conceived instead a plan for them to drive into Cheltenham one evening to attend one of the subscription dances, and had already inveigled her mama into giving her reluctant half-promise. Now she presented the plan as if it were all decided, saying merely, "I daresay it will not be half so good as anything in London, and the company will be far from select. But it will be amusing, and Lord knows there's little enough to do here in the evenings. Besides, there's my new ball dress that I haven't had a chance to wear yet, and it is vastly becoming, I promise you!"

Aunt Lela remained silent, though she was by no means in favor of the expedition. But she did cast a slightly anxious look at Sorrel, remembering her mourning. Sorrel had steadfastly refused to attend any balls or parties in London, and was equally determined not to make one (or rather sit bodkin) on a tiring journey to attend a ball she had no desire to go to.

But it would never occur to Livia to consider either her cousin or her mama's convenience, and she went on happily, "And we may indeed go to this tower tomorrow. You will like that, won't you, Mama, for you are forever talking of it. I daresay it will be a dead bore, but at least it will give us something to do, and we can go on horseback and have a picnic."

Aunt Lela looked even more doubtful, for she was more than slightly indolent, and would not have chosen to undertake so strenuous an expedition the day after she gave a dinner party. But again she made no protest.

"It sounds delightful," said his lordship, glancing quickly at Sorrel. "But is Miss Kent up to so much exertion so soon after her accident?"

Before Sorrel could deny any wish to play gooseberry for the afternoon, Livia answered carelessly for her, "Oh, then she may stay home with Mama! I doubt it would interest her anyway. And I have had an even more capital scheme! We may stay and drink tea in Broadway, and thus make a whole day of it." She seemed to have forgotten that the entire scheme had been designed for her mama's benefit.

It was again his lordship who intervened. "But then it was my understanding that the whole expedition was designed so that Mrs. Granville could see this tower again. But now that I come to think of it, she will scarcely wish to ride, so perhaps Miss Kent could accompany her in a carriage, and thus we may all go."

Livia cast Sorrel a rather venomous look, for she did not much care for this exaggerated concern for her unimportant cousin. But she was at least wise enough not to appear quite so churlish before her noble admirer. "Oh, yes. An excellent notion. Mama and Sorrel may drive, and we will meet them there. And then, if they do not care to stay so late, they may come back without us."

This was not exactly what his lordship had meant, as Sorrel well knew. But she also knew her cousin well enough, and her aunt as well, to expect that it would be exactly what would happen. Livia was no horsewoman, but she and her two admiring escorts would ride on ahead, enjoying themselves immensely, leaving Sorrel and her aunt to follow behind in a slow and stuffy carriage, bringing all the essentials for the picnic. It did indeed sound like a delightful plan. Sorrel only wished she might think of an excuse to remain behind, which would please Livia as well as herself, no doubt.

Chapter 8

But her aunt's dinner party was still to be gotten through first.

Sorrel, who retained a slight headache, would have been equally glad of an excuse to miss that, but there could be no thought of it with the vicar and his wife coming and several other wealthier members of the village. Sorrel knew her aunt was looking forward to the evening with unalloyed pleasure, for not only had she returned as a wealthy woman, and now might invite to dinner the very people who had snubbed her in her humbler days, but she could also boast the presence of a live marquis as a guest in her house, which would put the final seal on her happiness. Her cup, in fact, was in danger of running over completely.

It was otherwise with her daughter, who scarcely troubled to hide her boredom during the evening. Livia was slightly overdressed for so simple an occasion in an evening gown of white satin under an overdress of gold-shot gauze, and was in her best looks. But she was uninterested in such unfashionable locals, and would undoubtedly not have scrupled to monopolize the guest of honor had not his lordship forestalled her with a finesse it was a pleasure to watch.

In fact Sorrel had to reluctantly acknowledge that whatever Livia's manners might be, the marquis's were excellent. To all appearances he seemed delighted to hobnob with a set of people as dull as they were respectable, and showed himself not only not the least high in the instep, but very willing to be pleased. Whatever his secret thoughts about the evening might be, he disguised them so well that the female members of the party, at least, were all in danger of forming a decided partiality for him by the time the evening was over.

Even Lady Smythe, wife of the local squire and a starched-up dame in puce, with an imposing turban and a rather unpleasant titter, relaxed almost visibly in his presence. She had ample opportunity to do so, for despite all of her daughter's stormy representations, Aunt Lela for once had refused to give in, and it was Lady Smythe whom his lordship took in to dinner. However humble Aunt Lela's beginnings might have been, she was very well aware that Lady Smythe held precedence over a mere Miss Morden, and not all Livia's tears and threats succeeded in moving her.

Livia had to make do with Mr. FitzSimmons, who looked very distinguished and also made a considerable hit with the ladies. But since Lady Smythe was a stout female of no particular charm and even less tact, it was possible that his lordship was the greater sufferer.

But if so, Sorrel, watching him surreptitiously whenever she got the chance, was obliged to admit that he did not show it. He himself was looking ridiculously handsome in his evening clothes, and chatted politely with Lady Smythe, who under his charm was moved to something approaching animation; and with more obvious pleasure with his hostess on his other side, with whom he seemed to have struck up an unexpected understanding. If he cast any jealous glances to the opposite side of the table, where Livia was deliberately flirting outrageously with Mr. FitzSimmons, Sorrel at least did not discover it. But it seemed that there might indeed be times when his rank worked against him.

Aunt Lela, in even more imposing purple silk, and who had had to be gently restrained from emptying her jewel box in the very human wish to show off her wealth a little, was positively glowing, and obviously enjoying herself very much. She had greeted her old friends with pleasure and plainly was revelling so much in her return to Campden under such very different circumstances, that it was impossible to blame her. Even Lady Smythe was being unexpectedly kind to her.

For her part, Livia, wholly unhampered by such trifling considerations as good manners, ignored Sir Thomas Smythe on her other side to carry on a far too-lively conversation with a very willing Mr. FitzSimmons. Her mama cast her a worried glance or two, knowing full well Livia was showing herself at a disadvantage, for all her beauty. But Livia was never susceptible to hints, and seemed to be bent on shocking her mama's unfashionable friends as much as possible. Lady Smythe, for one, was looking daggers at her; but that might merely have been because her husband seemed to be lost in admiration of the vision of loveliness beside him.

Sorrel, learning more than even she wanted to know about the history of the village, which seemed to be a special interest of the vicar on her left, and forced to listen to Livia's silvery laughter across the table from her, could only conclude that the marquis's manners were indeed excellent. Either that, or else he was so sure of his superior claims that he had no need to feel jealous of a mere Mr. FitzSimmons.

The latter was undoubtedly true, but in light of their talk earlier that day, she at least hesitated to condemn him as easily as she might earlier have done. She had never before given the subject of rank much thought; but it seemed, like so much else, to be less simple than it first seemed. She could not help wondering how many dinner parties the marquis had been forced to sit through, making polite conversation to some wealthy and titled dowager, while his less noble fellows had the freedom to flirt with all the prettiest young females.

Of course, he must have the consolation of knowing perfectly well that he had only to throw down his gauntlet and it would be instantly picked up—by Livia certainly, and probably most other young ladies as well. But he was right that to be sought after merely because of his rank was scarcely a compliment.

She frowned unconsciously, a little startled at this quick change of tune in herself. Besides, she was being ridiculous. Stealing a peep at him, so handsome and polished and good-natured, it was impossible to believe he was sought after merely because he was a marquis. He would shine in any company.

Then Sorrel caught herself up short in annoyance. She was as bad as her cousin, for despite her instinctive prejudice she would seem to be in danger of falling victim to a handsome face and a charming smile.

She stole another glance at him, realizing that it was impossible to tell what he thought of the rather dull evening—or of her beautiful cousin for that matter. She still had no idea whether he was in love with Livia or not. When his eyes rested on her, which they did frequently, they showed undoubted appreciation, but he seemed unconcerned by the vision of his old friend flirting outrageously with her. She discovered that more and more she disliked the thought of him tying himself to the beautiful Livia for life.

Then he unexpectedly lifted his eyes and looked straight at Sorrel herself and smiled spontaneously. Flustered, she looked quickly away, annoyed to be caught staring like a schoolgirl, and fearful he might guess at her thoughts.

She was relieved when the ladies rose from the table. Unfortunately the gentlemen did not linger long over their port—no doubt on strict instructions from Aunt Lela.

When they came into the drawing room, conversation for the first time became general, and it was the kindly looking Mrs. Harris, the vicar's wife, an elderly lady of frail constitution but invigorating spirit, who said brightly, "Well, how delightful it is to meet again after all these years, and have the loose ends tied up. I always hate loose threads in one's life, don't you? Perhaps it comes of being a vicar's wife for so long, and believing myself in some part responsible for his flock. I remember the Harlaston girls, as I knew them then, very well of course, and followed their early career with interest. And to think we are all back here together again—or almost. But we have Miss Kent to represent her mama, and so it is almost the same."

"Aye, it is strange," agreed Aunt Lela with frank pride. "And if you'd asked me then if I'd come back someday to lease the biggest house in the neighborhood, I'd have said you was all about in your head. But I don't deny I've enjoyed myself more than I thought I would, revisiting old memories and old sights. I can't think why it took my niece's coming to bring me back."

"Oh, Mama," said Livia carelessly, "you know you hate the country in the general way. I am sure I don't blame you, for what anyone finds to do with themselves day after day is more than I can guess."

"Oh, we contrive to keep busy somehow," said Mrs. Harris with a twinkle in her eye. "But I daresay to a young girl it must seem decidedly flat—especially after your triumphs in London, Miss Morden. Your mama has been telling me about your success, my dear, and I'm sure it is no wonder. You put me strongly in mind—both you and your cousin do—of what your mama and her twin looked like at your age. And I believe they were the most beautiful girls I ever beheld in my life. It is amazing how it takes me back."

Livia looked pleased, for it was clear she quite rightly took the compliment entirely to herself, knowing Mrs. Harris was merely being polite to include Sorrel. But the vicar's wife's next words were less to her liking, for Mrs. Harris went on to say blithely, "But I am sure even the excitement of a London Season must appear tame to one used to a far more adventurous life. Miss Kent, I have been longing all evening to hear about life in America."

Sorrel, though she liked Mrs. Harris, was less pleased even than Livia to be thus singled out, and said unresponsively, "I fear it is not very different from life anywhere, ma'am."

"Oh, come, I will not believe that. The late unfortunate war—the vast distances—even the Red Indians that we hear so much about. I am sure it must be absolutely thrilling to live daily with so much adventure."

"You must excuse my wife, Miss Kent," said the vicar, a twinkle of his own in his elderly eyes. "She is fond of reading about distant places and loves to hear of them firsthand. I believe she always secretly wished me to become a missionary and go out among the cannibals in Africa."

"Oh, my dear! I am sure hearing about such adventures is the closest I would care to come to them. I fear I am not at all adventuresome myself. But I do enjoy hearing about distant places, as my husband says. I hope you will find the time to come to tea someday, Miss Kent, and indulge an old woman's weakness by telling me all about America."

Livia looked still less pleased that the invitation did not include herself, though she would never have wasted her time taking tea with an old woman. But Lady Smythe put in somewhat repressively, "For myself, I am sure it must be a most barbaric place, and I should not care to visit it, let alone live there. All those wars and rebellions and such! I am sure I do not know why they must forever be at loggerheads with us."

Sorrel was irritated, but knew it was pointless to try to rebut so sweeping an indictment, and held her tongue. But to her surprise it was the marquis who answered calmly—though with a twinkle in his own eyes, "Naturally I've no wish to appear disloyal to my own country, ma'am. But I believe in most cases the Americans had some right on their side."

Lady Smythe dismissed that easily. "Nonsense. I consider them all to be ungrateful traitors to the very country they owe their existence to. As for this latest war, I am out of all patience with them, and would be happy if we cut all ties to so upstart a country."

She appeared, belatedly, to realize that was scarcely polite, and added graciously, "I am sure I have nothing against Miss Kent, of course, for she can scarcely be held to blame for her country's excesses. After all, her mother is English." It was clear that in her eyes that outweighed a multitude of other sins.

Sorrel felt the betraying flush of anger in her cheeks, however foolish she knew it to be. "On the contrary, ma'am," she countered politely. "In general I do not like to boast of my connections, but I fear I am indeed to be considered at least partly to blame for my country's excesses, as you put it, since my grandfather was one of the Founding Fathers and voted in the Assembly for rebellion against Britain, and my father is a United States senator. My mother may have been English, but my sympathies are all with the American side, ma'am."

"Which is as it should be," said Mrs. Harris quickly.

Aunt Lela was looking flustered at this unexpected turn of events, but insisted loyally, "Indeed, my niece is something of a heroine herself, for she nursed a great many casualties during some battle or other, and was in a great deal of danger herself, so I understand."

Sorrel flushed still more hotly and was exceedingly sorry she had started the whole. But Lady Smythe was not yet finished. "Well!" she pronounced stiffly. "I am sure I meant no disrespect to Miss Kent. But I believe I am entitled to my own opinion."

"Exactly," said his lordship, looking at Sorrel with new interest. "Unless I am mistaken, that is exactly what the American revolution was fought over, ma'am. The right for every citizen to do and say exactly what he wishes."

Livia, long since bored with the conversation, interrupted brightly at that point, and with such unconscious rudeness that it was impossible to take offense. "Lord, why on earth are we talking of the American war? But I suppose I should be relieved Mama has not begged me to sing tonight, for she does in general, you know, however much I have asked her not to."

This hint was too broad to be ignored and effectively silenced the company completely. Mrs. Harris looked a little stunned at this demonstration of such supreme egotism, though the twinkle had returned to her eyes, and even Lady Smythe could find nothing to say. It was left to Mr. FitzSimmons, who exclaimed immediately, "By Jove, yes! You didn't think we were going to let you escape without entertaining us did you, Miss Morden?"

After a moment Mrs. Harris rather unsteadily added her pleas to Mr. FitzSimmons, and after a token protest that no one took in the least seriously, Livia was at last persuaded to play and sing for them. She played the piano indifferently, but her voice was better trained, and she looked so lovely that even Sir Thomas, no music lover, and who had at first looked a little pained at the suggestion, tapped his stick in time to the music and regarded Livia with rapt approval. Mr. FitzSimmons stood jealously at her elbow and turned the leaves of her music for her, and his lordship, for whom Livia's rather roguish ballad was obviously intended, gratified her by looking very well entertained.

Sorrel was happy to withdraw from the center of attention, though she could only regard her beautiful cousin with amazed respect. She should be used by now to her ruthless tactics, but it never ceased to amaze her how well they worked.

"Your cousin is very beautiful," remarked an amused voice in her ear. Sorrel looked round in surprise to find that Mrs. Harris had changed her seat for one beside her.

Sorrel was careful to keep her voice and face completely neutral. "Yes, very beautiful."

"And very determined. But I am glad to have this opportunity of speaking alone with you. I meant it that I hope you will drop in for tea with me sometime soon, my dear, if you can spare the time. I had a great fondness for your mother, you know, and would be happy to hear of her life after she left here."

Sorrel was grateful, if for no other reason than that someone else seemed to have seen through her cousin's tactics, and so said immediately, "Indeed, ma'am, and I am as anxious to hear of her life here. I would be delighted to come. She often speaks of this village, you know, and the people, including yourself and the vicar, who had treated her kindly."

Mrs. Harris looked pleased. "Does she? How very long ago it all seems, to be sure. She was the loveliest creature, you know. Quite bewitching, in fact."

Sorrel smiled slightly, too used to the statement to be offended. "I fear I do not much resemble her. Not as much as my cousin resembles my aunt."

Mrs. Harris's eyes twinkled again engagingly and she did not insult Sorrel's intelligence by denying it. "Perhaps not as much," she conceded, "though you have more the look of her than I think you realize. Your cousin is more like her, I will admit. Dear me, how it takes me back. All the local young men flocked around her like bees to honey, and it seemed to me she could twist them as easily around her finger as she did her pretty curls. Including Lady Smythe's own son, who made a complete cake of himself over your mother, did you know? Though I should not perhaps speak of it, especially since he is dead, poor boy. But to do him justice, although I always found him a most tedious young man, I honestly believe he would have married your mama in the face of his own mama's horrified opposition, if she would only have had him. Which fact undoubtedly is what is behind my old friend's somewhat thinly disguised animosity tonight, my dear. I hope you will disregard it."

Sorrel looked amused at this unexpected revelation.

"Indeed, ma'am, I am too used to it in this country to pay any attention to it," she said frankly. "I shouldn't have allowed her to goad me into a reply."

"My dear, I am glad you did. She deserves her come-uppance every now and then. It's odd, but in some ways you seem more like your aunt. Even as a girl Lela was by far the more practical and independent of the two. It doesn't surprise me in the least that she has outlived two wealthy husbands, for she always had an eye to the main chance—and I don't mean that at all in an unflattering way, believe me. But your mama. Tell me, my dear, did she ever regret going to America? I remember I was surprised to hear of it, at the time, for she seemed—well never mind. But do I take it her marriage with your father is happy?"

"Very happy, ma'am. And she has certainly not lost the knack of twisting men about her little finger, for my father is still very much in love with her. As for regretting coming to America, I can only say that I can scarcely remember a time when she didn't have at least half a dozen young men madly in love with her, and she is considered the most noted hostess in Washington."

"Ah, yes, that sounds like her," said Mrs. Harris in amusement. "But if you don't mind my saying so, my dear, I am not sure I would have cared to have a mother who was always the belle of the ball. I hope you are not offended by my frankness?"

After a moment Sorrel said dryly, "No, I am not offended. I daresay it's true that she is not—not very motherly. But I assure you I love her dearly for all that. As you also see, I did not inherit her beauty, and that has caused—some problems. When I was a child it scarcely mattered, for I adored her as everyone else did, and it never occurred to me to—to compete with her. Oh, that sounds horrid, and I don't mean it to. Besides, there was never any question of my being able to compete with her—any more than there is with my cousin now." She smiled a little to take any bitterness out of her words. "I learned early, you see, for even Papa has never had eyes for anyone else when my mother is in the room. And I can't think why I am telling you all this, ma'am!"

Mrs. Harris squeezed her hand warmly. "Because you have needed someone to talk to, and perhaps because I am a stranger, and knew your mama a little. I think you are too used to hiding your light under a bushel, as we used to say." She indicated Sorrel's gray gown, even more somber in contrast to Livia's expensive confection. "I see you have also recently suffered a bereavement."

Sorrel's eyes unexpectedly misted, and she blinked hurriedly, embarrassed by the show of emotion. She wondered if she would ever become accustomed to talking of it. "My—my fiancé. He was killed in the late war."

"Oh, my dear! I am so very sorry. That makes what I am going to say next even more improper. But for all your intelligence, my dear, you are mistaken about one thing at least," she said calmly. "I will not insult you by trying to make you believe you are as beautiful as your cousin. But you are more competition to her than you perhaps know. Why else has the marquis—such a handsome man—I declare I am half in love with myself, and in general, you know, I am no great lover of titles—scarcely taken his eyes from you all evening?"

Chapter 9

Sorrel felt her heart jump foolishly, and then made herself be sensible. "That—you must be mistaken, ma'am," she said quickly.

"Am I? I suspect that playing second fiddle to your mama all your life has made you less than aware of your own very real charm, my dear."

"Perhaps," said Sorrel, not believing it.

It was clear Mrs. Harris saw that, for she did not try to press it. Instead she said even more surprisingly, "Having gone so far, I will go even further and say that I would be careful, if I were you, my dear."

"Be *careful*?" Sorrel belatedly realized her voice was too sharp, and strove to modify it. "Why on earth did you say that, ma'am?"

"Oh, dear. My husband would be cross with me, for I am sure I am being very indiscreet," said that lady ruefully. "But at my age one grows tired of always being discreet. I only meant that it is obvious to one of my years that your cousin is very used to getting her own way, and I would not personally like to stand in the path of anything she wants. There, that is cutting up a character finely, is it not? And when I am a guest in your aunt's home as well."

But Sorrel had relaxed a little, able to dismiss that easily. For a moment she had been wholly startled, thinking the vicar's wife must know something of the threat against her aunt. But that Livia could ever think she had anything to fear from her American cousin was ludicrous. "I think you mean to be kind, ma'am, but you are mistaken. Oh, not that my cousin dislikes competition, but that she has anything to fear from me. For some reason it amuses his lordship to—to tease me, but that is all it is, I promise you."

She glanced unwittingly to her cousin as she spoke, and saw Mr. FitzSimmons standing attentively at her elbow, and Lord Wycherly at no great distance, both clearly engrossed in the performance and looking more than appreciative at the lovely picture she made.

Mrs. Harris followed her glance, and remarked somewhat dryly, "Well, I will not dispute with you, my dear, though that is not precisely the way I read the situation. But there, the music is over, and we must take our leave, for neither my husband nor I am used to late hours any longer, I fear. How convenient that we live but a few steps from your lodge gates. I hope you will be able to forgive an old busybody, for my only excuse is that I knew your mother. It would give an old woman a great deal of pleasure if you could avail yourself of my invitation, for I would love to further our acquaintance."

Sorrel thanked her, accepting the invitation with genuine pleasure, even if she could not help wondering what else the remarkable Mrs. Harris might say. But there was indeed time for no more, for the vicar rose, making his excuses, and the party broke up.

If Sorrel once again went to bed with a great deal to think about, and lay awake for some hours, she was at least thankful that no one need know but herself.

She was able, without too much consideration, to dismiss Mrs. Harris's words as the product of an old and obviously warmhearted woman's romantic imaginings. Sorrel had been too long in her own mother's shadow to imagine that his lordship might find her anything but an amusing diversion. If he had looked at her during the evening—though with her cousin there she found that very difficult to believe—she had no doubt it was merely in the mocking way he had adopted for her, as if for some reason he found her secretly entertaining. Or perhaps he still suspected her of having set her cap for him.

That thought was enough to put an angry sparkle in her eyes, for she was not on the catch for a rich or titled husband. But what kept her awake long after that flush of anger had died down, and was the cause of considerable soul-searching, was the shameful realization of how much, in that first instant, she had wanted it to be true.

Well, if that was the way the wind was blowing, then the more fool she, and the sooner she got hold of herself the better. It was no doubt ironic in the extreme that having resisted the appeal of all the young men who flocked about her mother, making great cakes of themselves, she should find herself absurdly attracted to a man who epitomized everything she had always held in contempt. She was a democrat and he was a marquis, sought after and kowtowed to for no reason but his noble title. With the exception of William, she had failed to attract attention from even the plainest of young men at home, and he was both charming and remarkably handsome, and admitted that he was the object of every ambitious young lady in England. The thing was ridiculous on its face.

Finally—and it kept coming back to this—despite Mrs. Harris's words Sorrel knew she stood not a chance of competing with her beautiful cousin Livia. Even if she could, it would be an act of ultimate betrayal toward the aunt who had been kind to her to steal him from her cousin. She could not do it.

That last thought made her laugh a little bitterly, for nothing was less likely. Why on earth, she deliberately lashed herself, did she imagine he would look twice at her, with her beautiful cousin nearby—especially when any number of men with far less to offer than he had looked straight through her?

Being naturally honest, she could come up with no reason whatsoever. Unless, of course, he was using her to make Livia jealous in his turn.

The thought had her frowning in the dark, for she was

a little surprised at how much she disliked the notion. And yet it might explain a great deal. He must know perfectly well that Livia was using Mr. FitzSimmons in an attempt to make him jealous and force him into a declaration. It might very well amuse him to give her a little of her own back again by flirting with her plain American cousin.

If so, that was clearly even more of a reason for Sorrel herself to stand back, for she had no wish to be used for so base a purpose. Besides, no more than Mrs. Harris did she underestimate her cousin's capacity for jealousy. They might very well carry on their unpleasant little courtship without involving her.

All the same, she could not help wondering what on earth had given Mrs. Harris, who seemed an astute woman, the absurd notion that his lordship had been staring at her all night. The few times Sorrel had allowed herself to glance in his direction, he had seemed either engaged with his dinner partner or looking at her beautiful cousin, which was only to be expected.

And it was beyond foolishness to waste even a second wishing that for once in her life it might have been otherwise, and she the beautiful, vivacious center of attention. If nothing else she had hoped she had long since outgrown such useless envy.

Under the circumstances, it was hardly surprising that Sorrel heartily hoped for pouring rain the next day, which might prevent the proposed expedition to the tower. But when she opened her curtains early the next morning, it was to find a beautiful June day, with not a cloud in the sky and every promise of being perfect for a picnic.

Since there was no getting out of it, she went down early to check again on the chestnut. She was just straightening from feeling his knees when a by now far too familiar voice said behind her, "I thought I would find you here again, Miss Kent."

She jerked around too rapidly, then took a firm hold of herself, annoyed both at her pleasure and her unexpected shyness. "I—good morning, my lord."

"How is the chestnut?" he inquired sympathetically.

"The limp seems to have gone, thank goodness," she answered, grateful for so safe a topic. "I am only thankful he did not do himself a permanent injury."

"But then your aunt assures me that her third husband has little room for complaint even if he had," he said in amusement. "I like her very much, by the way. In fact I wish I might have seen the two of them together so long ago, for Mrs. Granville assures me they were all the rage, which I can readily believe. Is your mother very like her?"

This topic was less to Sorrel's liking. "In looks, yes," she said briefly, "but not in personality. But excuse me, my lord. My aunt will be looking for me."

"I doubt it, for she was still at the breakfast table when I left her. And we were interrupted yesterday before we could finish our talk, remember," he reminded her politely. "I certainly seem to have exchanged scarcely a word with you last night."

She strove to make her voice sound light and unconcerned, though such a "talk" was the last thing she desired. "Why, I thought we had said all there was to say, my lord. I am grateful for your concern, but I must confess I cannot take your warning seriously. I can't imagine why anyone would wish to harm me."

He was frowning a little and regarding her in a manner that she found far too close for comfort. "Nor can I, Miss Kent," he said at last. "But nevertheless, I assure you I did not make it up. Tell me, is this your famous American sangfroid speaking, or do you have some reason for doubting my word?"

This was even worse than she had feared, but she had no choice but to continue. "Of course not. It is not a question of doubting your word, my lord. But I have been in England less than a month, and I am not aware of having made any enemies in so short a time. Unless, of course, it is Lady Smythe, who dislikes all Americans, and whose son was once in love with my mother, so the vicar's wife informs me. But I hardly think she would go so far as to sabotage my girth."

His brows had drawn even closer together and his eyes were uncomfortably penetrating. "I see," he said dryly at last. "I cannot decide whether you are very brave, Miss Kent—or very foolish. But you have made one thing perfectly clear. For whatever reason, you have deliberately chosen not to trust me. Whether that is due to your absurd prejudice against my rank, or for some other reason I have no idea. But you confirm for me what was merely a suspicion before."

"And what is that?" she demanded warily.

"Why that when I informed you yesterday of what had happened, you were clearly startled. But you were not surprised, Miss Kent. You were not in the least surprised."

She felt the betraying flush, but said quickly, "Now you are being ridiculous, my lord. I have already told you I can think of no one who could have a reason to wish me harm. I took a toss, that's all. Unfortunately I have taken many before that, and I am sure shall take many more. Surely there is no need for all this mystery?"

He shrugged. "I wonder if your aunt would agree with you?"

That caught her off guard. "Good Lord," she exclaimed unwisely, "I hope you did not tell my aunt so ridiculous a rigmarole!"

"No, I respected your obvious wish for secrecy—at least for the moment. But I warn you, my dear Miss Kent, that despite your brave attempt to pull the wool over my eyes, I am not quite so great a fool as you obviously believe me, even though I am an aristocrat. And whether you trust me or not, I reserve the right to keep an eye on you for myself. For if I am right, you are in a great deal of danger, whether you wish to admit it or not."

Sorrel did her best to dismiss his words during the long afternoon that followed, though without much success. More than ever she would gladly have gotten out of going on the proposed expedition if she could, but it was true that Aunt Lela had been looking forward to seeing the tower again. Besides, Sorrel had little doubt that Livia would take good care to keep both of her suitors firmly at her side. Not one to share her beaux, was her beautiful cousin Livia. Or to take pity on those females less fortunate and sought-after than she.

In fact, Sorrel fully expected her cousin to fulfill her threat to gallop off with both men, leaving her mama and cousin to bring up the rear unescorted. It would not even occur to her to consider their feelings in the matter, or remember that her mother did not like to go anywhere without male protection.

And so it quickly became apparent that was what Livia intended. But it seemed that both she and Sorrel had again reckoned without his lordship.

For the marquis, though attentive to Livia in his charming way, firmly scuttled from the outset any plan to ride off and leave the barouche to follow. To Livia's ingenuous explanation that her mama would not mind in the least, and besides, it would be deadly dull to be plodding along in the wake of the carriage, especially on so hot a day, he answered blandly, and with his most delightful smile, "Then you and Fitz go on ahead, Miss Morden. I assure you I do not mind in the least plodding, as you put it. And besides, I would not for the world leave your mother and your cousin to travel alone."

This, of course, was not in the least what her cousin wanted, and Livia frowned and said even more carelessly, "Oh, Mama does not mind! Do you, Mama?"

Aunt Lela, whose views on the folly of helpless women traveling anywhere alone were well known to her daughter, swallowed, obviously torn between gratification toward his lordship for this show of good manners, and the desire to please her daughter. The latter won in the end, as it usually did. "No, indeed," she said valiantly. "I am sure the coachman knows the way, and besides, we are unlikely to meet with any danger in the middle of the afternoon. You go ahead and enjoy yourself, my lord, for I am sure you must be longing for a gallop."

But Lord Wycherly, apparently immune either to hints or to the darkling looks cast him by the fulminating beauty at his side, again assured her that he was quite content with his company. As if to prove it, he immediately began to make civil conversation with his hostess, as if that were the end of the discussion.

Livia, unused to having her wishes so patently ignored, was left fuming, and immediately began to pay him back by flirting outrageously in turn with Mr. FitzSimmons, who was nothing loath. Thus the party made its desultory way for some time, the marquis riding abreast of the carriage and conversing with its occupants—or rather, with Aunt Lela, for Sorrel remained steadfastly silent—and seemingly oblivious to the other two, who drew gradually farther and farther ahead, and seemed to be enjoying themselves immensely, if their laughter was anything to go by.

Sorrel was torn between secret amusement and dismay by the whole charade. At least if he married her cousin, it seemed clear that his lordship would be master in his own home. Livia might find her much-sought-after title came at a greater price than she had anticipated.

But if the marquis was indeed fulfilling his threat to keep an eye on Sorrel, that was far less amusing, of course. She was honor-bound not to tell him the truth, but she placed increasingly less reliance on his being so easily fobbed off—especially after seeing him handle her cousin so effectively.

Livia, for her part, took her revenge by ignoring his

lordship completely. Sorrel had no doubt that such tactics had worked well for her in the past, but she was beginning to doubt they would work with his lordship. The
spoiled beauty might well have mistaken her man for
once.

Then again, perhaps not. Livia was no horsewoman,
as Sorrel well knew, but she was dressed in a vastly becoming habit of celestial blue, with a daring hat adorned
with a number of curling plumes set on her golden head,
and she looked so delightful that few would bother to
notice that her mount was far from mettlesome and in
general she preferred any other mode of exercise than a
good gallop. If the marquis was aware that Livia was
once more showing herself in a far from flattering light,
his attitude toward her remained one of amused and tol-
erant admiration.

Mr. FitzSimmons, also, was clearly besotted, and for
his part soon took advantage of his unexpected luck to
coax Livia off the road to follow some shortcut that he
knew of. The first thing the rest of the party knew about
it was when Livia, seemingly in high good spirits by
then, though still with a malicious gleam in her eyes,
rode back to inform her mama of this change in plan.
"For Mr. FitzSimmons says he knows of a shortcut," she
said blithely. "We shall be able to get there much
quicker, and will make the arrangements for us all, for
you know how much you dislike delays, Mama."

Aunt Lela looked doubtful, for she did not much like
Livia going off without a chaperon. Sorrel knew that her
aunt was very conscious of her own social disadvan-
tages, and was convinced that because of it Livia must
be more circumspect than someone better born, and
about whom malicious gossip could not be so damaging.
But she was far too good-natured—and knew her daughter too well—to risk refusing her permission.

It was equally clear that Livia believed that would be
enough to bring the marquis to heel. But if so, she was
again mistaken, for he merely said teasingly, "Take care,

Miss Morden, that Fitz here don't lead you astray! He's hopelessly unreliable where directions are concerned. I confess I would not like to follow one of his so-called shortcuts."

Mr. FitzSimmons, who had also reined in to join them, protested indignantly at that slur, and Livia, after another challenging look at the marquis, tossed her head and became again vivacious, and a little scornful. "Oh, well," she said, "at least we shall have had an adventure. I am sure there is nothing more tedious than to plod along and play propriety. Coming, Mr. FitzSimmons? We shall be there ages before you can reach the place by road."

Sorrel for once privately agreed with her cousin, for she found the slow pace of the carriage amazingly tedious. But she again watched in mingled amusement and reluctant respect as his lordship merely smiled and refused to be drawn. "Then we shall see you there," he said cheerfully.

Chapter 10

Livia kicked her horse and rudely left them in a cloud of dust, clearly in a furious mood that did not bode well for the rest of the afternoon. But Mr. FitzSimmons, as always, was more urbane. He grinned somewhat ruefully at his friend, assured his hostess that the shortcut was indeed safe, and that he would take the utmost care of her daughter, and then touched his whip to his hat in a brief salute, and more decorously followed.

Sorrel, who happened to be sitting (to her earlier annoyance) in the side of the open barouche nearest to his lordship, could not resist taking advantage of her aunt addressing some question to the coachman to say mockingly under her breath, "Unwise, my lord! Perhaps I should warn you that my cousin will not tolerate many such defections."

He merely smiled down at her. "Do you think so?" was all he could be brought to admit. "I can only repeat, I am perfectly happy with my company." Then he turned to answer a question from her aunt, and the subject was dropped.

Sorrel was left to consider the matter for the rest of the journey. Absurd though it might be, it seemed that he had indeed constituted himself in some part her guardian, though she could not imagine why. Probably, she told herself firmly, his actions were prompted by no more than chivalry. Or perhaps he was merely furthering his own plot to pay Livia back in her own coin.

Though that thought pleased Sorrel even less, if it was

indeed part of his plan to keep Livia guessing, he was succeeding admirably. He blew first hot then cold; and even Sorrel, who had gotten into the habit of watching him closely whenever he was unaware of her scrutiny, was still no wiser as to what his intentions were toward her beautiful cousin. It almost began to seem as if Livia had met her match at last.

They arrived at the tower before Sorrel was able to reach a satisfactory answer to either question. The only thing that was abundantly clear was that the noble Marquis of Wycherly was likely to throw a considerable wrench into her own plans, and cause unnecessary trouble between the cousins, if she let him.

Livia and Mr. FitzSimmons were there before them, and, as promised, already had made arrangements to visit the privately owned tower. Livia still looked to be in a dangerous mood, and strolled out to greet them, the tail of her habit thrown carelessly over her arm, and complaining of the length of time the barouche had taken, the heat of the day, and that having now seen the famous tower, she was convinced it had been a waste of their time in coming.

Sorrel was herself heartily sick of the entire expedition by then, but she could only watch in admiration the way his lordship proceeded to charm Livia out of her sulks. Somehow, in what manner Sorrel was never afterward able to say, he subtly took charge of the afternoon, establishing his hostess in a shady spot where she could doze a little, and convincing the fractious Livia to climb the tower with the rest of them. In this he was ably assisted by Mr. FitzSimmons, who looked quietly amused, and for once seemed content to leave the difficult beauty to more experienced hands.

Livia, almost visibly blossoming under this flattering attention, forgot her earlier grievances, and even made no objection to the ancient rustic who served both as caretaker and guide, and who, brightening visibly at sight of their party, hurried into his jacket. Visitors were rare, and it soon became apparent that he was not going to allow them to omit any part of the tower's history or attractions.

He pointed out that Fish Hill, where the tower stood, had been a beacon point for centuries, and probably a fire had burned there to warn of the approaching Spanish Armada. The tower itself was built by the Sixth Earl of Coventry in the 1790s on part of his Spring Hill estate and had been designed by the famous architect James Wyatt, who had also built Kew Palace. The earl also owned Croome Court about twelve miles to the north, and the tower was frequently used as a signaling station to let Croome Court know when the family was on its way from Spring Hill.

Livia, already growing bored, at least had the grace to remark under her breath that he might have hired a footman for a great deal less money.

But the guide, despite his advanced age, seemed to have excellent hearing, for he said promptly, "Aye, miss, but 'tis a folly, ye ken, and 'tis believed the earl's second wife was behind the building of it. They say she used it often as a vantage point to give a view of the chase when there was a hunt on the estate. She would entertain the ladies here, and then they would gather for a picnic after the hunt was done. Ye'll be wanting to climb to the top, o' course, for that's why everyone comes. The view is grand from there, and on a clear day, like today, ye can see seven counties."

Livia still eyed the tall tower with some misgiving, clearly thinking the view of seven counties hardly worth the climb; but Aunt Lela said at once, "Oh, yes, you must climb to the top, for the view from there is striking! It was new-built when I was a girl, and I remember well driving over to look at it. Your mama and I, my dear, climbed to the top and swore we could see our own home even," she said to Sorrel. "Dear me, how long ago that seems now. I am tempted to try it myself, only that I am grown too old and stout, I fear, to risk it. But you must go up by all means."

His lordship said in amusement, "I hope you do not mean to disappoint me after coming all this way, Miss Morden?" Unfortunately he then somewhat undermined his recent success by adding with a frown, "Though I am by no means so sure Miss Kent should make the attempt, after her recent accident."

Livia's eyes narrowed again, for she did not like anyone else to get attention but herself. But she merely said ungraciously, "I am not sure any of us should make the attempt, but it would be ridiculous if my cousin did not make the climb since it was her idea to come in the first place."

She made it seem as if Sorrel had dragged them all there for her own amusement. But after a moment his lordship shrugged. "Very well. We shall duly report to you, ma'am, whether the view is as good as it was when you used to come here."

The climb up the narrow circular stairs was indeed a breathless one, particularly on so hot a day, and Livia complained that the stone walls were marking her expensive habit. There were, as the guide had told them, octagonal rooms at each level, furnished as sitting rooms, and looking amazingly comfortable. But to Sorrel at least, the view at the top was dramatic enough to more than repay the climb.

Forgetting the others, she went to the stone railing, entranced to find all of the Cotswolds laid out below her. If she could not make out seven counties, it was even more enjoyable to think that her mother had seen the same view so long ago, and perhaps found it as entrancing as Sorrel did herself.

Livia, however, predictably grew quickly bored, and wandered away from the edge in a very few minutes, preparatory to going down again. She had firmly snared the marquis and clearly did not mean to let him escape again. Her hand on his arm and her ill temper apparently forgotten, she was talking animatedly to him. Mr. FitzSimmons, too, seemed ready to go down, and was observing his chief rival with an expression it was difficult to interpret.

The marquis, however, halted at the door to the stairs, and ignoring his companion's chatter for the moment, said calmly, "One moment! We cannot leave your cousin alone up here. Miss Kent? Are you ready to go down yet?"

Sorrel looked around quickly, and saw that they were all waiting for her. "No, go on without me," she said quickly. "I shall be down in a moment or two."

His lordship looked doubtful, but then shrugged, and Livia pulled him away with a laughing comment that Sorrel did not doubt was at her expense. She deliberately ignored it and turned back to the view, and shortly thereafter heard the door to the stairs close, and the voices cut off.

She was relieved to find herself alone. On the top of the windy tower, with the whole of the green country laid out before her, looking from that height like some lilliputian land, with the towns and houses reduced to the size of toys, and the rivers no more than wavy silver lines, she felt she could have drunk in the view forever. It was no wonder her mother and aunt had been intrigued with it when they were young, and she was glad despite everything that she had come. She would like to make the trip again alone and without distractions, so that she could get her fill of the solitude and the view.

But oddly, it was not of this tame and green land that she was thinking, as she stood there gazing out somewhat blindly. She felt a powerful and unexpected connection with this country of her mother's, but perhaps it had been a mistake to come after all. Everything was suddenly too complicated, and for the first time since she'd left she felt as homesick as a little girl, longing to be back where at least she understood who she was and what her role was.

But of course that had changed at home, as well. William was dead and there would be no marriage now. And though she may not have loved him in the way she perhaps should have, at least her future had been settled. Now everything was up in the air again. This time in England had been a way of avoiding the future, she saw now, but she could not afford to hide from reality for very long. Soon she must go home and perhaps at last come to terms with everything the marriage with William had allowed her to avoid. And if for some reason she now felt more mixed up than ever, and was having difficulty even bringing William's face to mind, that was something she did not want to reflect on.

She did not realize there were tears on her cheeks until she heard a faint sound behind her. She turned slowly, not even surprised by then to find the marquis calmly waiting for her.

Even so, she started and exclaimed foolishly, "I thought you had gone, my lord!"

"And wished I had, by the expression on your face. But I warned you, did I not, that I was going to keep a close eye on you."

This was taking his threat to keep an eye on her to a ridiculous degree! Her embarrassment at being found out again in so foolish a situation found outlet in anger. "This is ridiculous, my lord! Did you really imagine some villain would be lurking up here to throw me off?" She glanced mockingly around the small, windswept aerie, which provided no possible hiding place. "That is as absurd as your remaining behind today to guard me from wholly imaginary dangers, and it has got to stop!"

He shrugged. "It seems you leave me no other choice. For some reason you choose not to acknowledge the danger you may be in, Miss Kent. You obviously need someone to look after you."

She was wholly exasperated. "I don't understand you in the least! Even if I were in danger, we are strangers, and you are jeopardizing your position with my cousin.

Besides, why would I try to hide such a thing if it were true? It makes no sense. I begin to think you have indeed been a soldier too long, and imagine enemies behind every bush."

"Why you would try to hide it from me is what I am trying to discover," he countered a touch grimly. "And I must confess I am beginning to have my own ideas on the subject."

That had her frowning, but she did not think he could possibly guess the truth. She said impatiently, "Pray let us go down, my lord. My aunt—and my cousin—will be wondering what has become of us."

He stood before the door to the stairs, but he still did not immediately open it. "In a moment, Miss Kent," he said. Then he added mockingly at her revealing expression, "Don't look so alarmed. I have never been one to pursue a forlorn hope, and I have no intention of pressing you any further on a subject you are so strangely reticent on."

"I am not in the least alarmed!" she insisted indignantly, and not wholly truthfully.

He ignored that. "I have said I have no intention of pursuing the matter at the moment, Miss Kent. Though I should perhaps warn you that I have indeed been a soldier too long to be gulled by a mere feint, however cleverly designed. But I begin to think I have an even more important question to ask of you."

She was full of wariness, and even further from understanding him or his motives. "I can't imagine what that could be," she said defiantly.

"Can't you, Miss Kent?" he inquired ruefully. "I feared I was more transparent than that. Who is William?"

Chapter 11

Her breath caught, for he had once again managed to take her wholly by surprise. She turned away quickly, to hide the recurrence of the foolish tears, and repeated as if she had never heard the name before, "William?"

"Yes. You called me by his name after your fall."

"Did I?" She remembered her first foolish confusion. "He was my—fiancé."

"Was?"

She swallowed, for she still did not like to talk of it. "Yes. He, too, was a—soldier, and was killed during the attack on Fort McHenry." She added starkly after a moment, for some reason she couldn't understand, "He died in my arms."

"I'm sorry," he said gently. Without warning he turned her back to face him and touched the wetness on her cheek. "You must have loved him very much."

"Yes," she said simply, for it was true, if not in the way he meant. They had been friends, not lovers, but she still missed him. Though she wondered if the tears had really been for William, earnest, uncomplicated William, dead too soon in a war he had been so eager to enter, or for herself, left to pick up the pieces and go on.

"I—see," he said at last. "Forgive me."

She doubted that he did, but lifted her head with pride. "It would be foolish to say it doesn't matter. But it happened almost a year ago, and life goes on. You must know that as well as anyone."

"Yes, it goes on."

She suddenly wanted to put an end to a tête-à-tête in which she knew herself to be wholly out of her depth, and too vulnerable at the moment to resist him. "My aunt will be waiting," she said again. "Please—let us go down."

"Very well, Miss Kent." This time he opened the door for her immediately. But when she would have hurried through, he said abruptly, "Wait. Let me go down first. The stairs are very steep."

He went before her down the stairs, and she followed quickly. But her anxiety to rejoin the others proved her undoing in the end. She was halfway down the first turn when her foot caught in the hem of her skirt, and before she could prevent herself she pitched forward down the steep and narrow stairs.

She would undoubtedly have suffered a nasty fall had he not possessed such quick reflexes. The cry had barely escaped her lips when he had caught her, and held her safely, his strong arms wholly supporting her while she regained her balance.

He did not immediately release her, even after she had regained her footing. Her heart was pounding out of all proportion to the danger, and she discovered, to her shame, that she liked the feel of his arms about her far too much. It was not the first time he had made her feel delicate and fragile, when she knew she was not. But it was a dangerous and insidious feeling that she must resist at all costs. "I—thank you," she said breathlessly. "I don't know how I came to be so clumsy."

"You would seem to be accident-prone, Miss Kent," he remarked. "That is twice that I have saved your life. I begin to think you need a permanent keeper."

But that was ridiculous, and at least succeeded in bringing her back down to earth. She pulled abruptly away and said sharply, "In any event, you cannot blame this on some mysterious enemy, for it was nothing but my own stupid clumsiness. Besides, in neither case would I have done more than suffer a few scrapes and bruises. My life was scarcely in danger."

She stood on the steep step above him, and he still kept a hold on her arms, so that they were standing uncomfortably close, her face almost on a level with his. She saw that for once his very blue eyes were almost wholly devoid of humor. "I will not even bother to ask if all Americans are as stubborn as you, Miss Kent, for I should know by now that you are a law unto yourself. You seem willfully determined to make light of two incidents that might have ended in serious injury or even death. In this case, though I don't indeed suspect anything more than undue carelessness on your part in your haste to get away from me, I suspect you would have suffered a little more than a few scrapes and bruises. You might even have broken your mulish little neck on these damnably steep stairs—which would undoubtedly amply repay you for refusing to confide in me. But though I can't force you to trust me—we are strangers, after all, as you so correctly point out, and I am an aristocrat to boot—I will promise you two things, my dear Miss Kent."

"And what are they?" she demanded warily.

He smiled down at her with his sudden, charming smile, the uncustomary frown fading away. "Why, that you shall confide in me before this is over, and of your own free will, too," he said confidently.

She did not believe it. There were too many things that stood between them. "And the other?"

Abruptly he lifted her chin with one finger and made her look at him. "That I shall make you trust me as well," he said. "If for no other reason than to prove to you that I am not the fashionable fribble you so clearly think me. You might say my *amour propre* is at stake, Miss Kent. You are not the only one with an excess of pride and a liking to think herself invincible."

Then he released her and without another word started down the stairs again. Sorrel followed him automatically, in more danger of falling and breaking her neck now, had he but known it, than earlier, for she was wholly unaware of the steepness of the stairs and could not feel her feet on them.

The rest of the picnic at least passed off without a hitch. The marquis, as if to make up for his earlier neglect, firmly attached himself to her beautiful cousin, and set himself to win her back to good humor. He succeeded so well that her silvery laugh sounded often, and Aunt Lela, who had been looking slightly puzzled, relaxed, and confided to Sorrel contentedly what a handsome couple they made.

There could be no disputing that. Livia, in her blue habit and daring hat, looked so beautiful that it was no wonder his lordship seemed to have eyes only for her; and he himself, with his blond good looks and charm of manner was a perfect complement for her. No one, seeing them laughing together, with their heads so close, could doubt that two such golden and supremely confident beings were right for each other. Even Mr. FitzSimmons, who cast them one or two jealous glances, seemed resigned, and devoted himself to Aunt Lela.

Livia, reveling in her noble suitor's undivided attention for once, ordered him about with a pretty imperiousness, having him fetch her parasol for her, for the sun was in her eyes, and then to move her cushion a little way away from the rest, for it was so deliciously cool in the shade. She looked smugly aware of her own powers, and once she had succeeded in getting him a little apart, engaged him in low-voiced conversation, wholly ignoring the others.

Sorrel, to her own self-disgust, could not keep her eyes from straying in that direction, and watched with dislike as her cousin talked animatedly to him, looking her sparkling loveliest, while his handsome head was bent a little to hear what she was saying. She would not admit that the emotion she herself was feeling was jealousy, but again it occurred to her that it would be a shame if her cousin did indeed succeed in attaching the marquis. He was too nice a man for her cousin's coils.

That brought her up with a start, for she did not like the direction her thoughts were taking. Her first loyalty should be to her cousin. Or at least her aunt. But with a little frown between her brows, she searched in vain for any signs of love, or even affection toward her noble suitor in her beautiful cousin's face. All that she could find was a secret look of triumph. Livia's eyes were full of his coronet, and it was doubtful that she even saw him at all, however handsome and charming he might be.

As for his lordship, Sorrel still was far from believing Mrs. Harris's extraordinary statement, but she was at a loss to understand what game he might be playing with her. That he could be interested in her with her beautiful cousin nearby was beyond crediting. And that being the case, it was foolish beyond permission to dwell too much on the things he had said, or on the unexpected flame in his very blue eyes when he had looked at her. That way could only lay disaster.

Besides, there could be perfectly logical reasons for his unexpected conduct, though she was at something of a loss to guess them. But then he had said he regretted being obliged to sell out. Perhaps he was indeed bored, and found in the mystery of her cut girth nothing more than an outlet for his pent-up energy.

Yes, that made some sort of sense, at least. But if so, it was likely to make the next week or so even more difficult, for she was coming to have a grudging respect for his tenacity, if nothing else. He was the one person her aunt did not wish to know of the blackmail attempt, but it might not be so easy after all to pull the wool over his eyes. He had said he would not pursue forlorn hopes, which hopefully meant that he would no longer press his inconvenient and uncomfortable questions upon her. But it did not seem in the least likely that she had managed to lull his suspicions. Or that he would be willing to let it go at that. His absurd insistence upon keeping a close eye on her all day, to her cousin's obvious fury, argued that fact all too well.

In fact, he was becoming a distinct nuisance, and she wished he would go and play his chivalrous games elsewhere. It was all absurd, and not the least because, however sure he might be of his final conquest of her cousin, his championing of Sorrel herself was doing the relationship between the cousins no good at all. For all his talk of the drawbacks of his title, he must know perfectly well that however fast and loose he might play with her, Livia would be his for the mere lifting of a finger. And if Sorrel had seen no sign that he was in turn in love with her cousin, he must have meant to offer for her when he came, for everyone accepted that was so.

Unfortunately, Livia had once or twice that day given Sorrel a sharp glance that did not bode well for the future. And though it was unlikely Livia could ever consider Sorrel a serious rival, a schism between them could only cause Aunt Lela unhappiness. In fact, his lordship's lighthearted amusing himself with the mystery was likely to cause far more harm than he could possibly guess.

He had also said—in fact almost threatened—that he would make her trust him in the end, but she did not foresee it. Too much lay between them, and if his charming smile was too apt to linger in her memory, despite all she could do to eradicate it, why then, the more fool she. It would be beyond folly to trust the noble Marquis of Wycherly. Or to put any stock in the things he said.

Livia had stubbornly clung to the notion they should stop off in Broadway to have tea on their way back, but in light of his lordship's earlier stubbornness, she did not again suggest that her mother and cousin might return without them. Sorrel herself thought it an excellent idea, however.

But she was not really surprised when, despite her aunt's obvious tiredness after the long day, they retired to the White Hart for tea in the lovely village nearby, as

Livia wanted. Or that the entire party went, despite Livia's own preferences in the matter. It seemed that her cousin and the marquis were well suited in more than looks, for they were both obviously adept at getting their own way.

Nothing could have exceeded the graciousness of their reception at this famous and ancient hostelry. They were bowed into a private parlor, and the ladies conducted upstairs to a bedchamber, low-ceilinged and obviously ancient, to refresh themselves and repair the damage caused by fresh wind and exercise, before they rejoined the gentlemen.

Aunt Lela, plainly revived and enjoying herself, remarked that she had once been there as a child, and how much it took her back. But Livia, once away from his lordship, abandoned the cheerful manner completely. She scowled and complained as she primped her hair and removed any signs of the effect of wind and dust from her appearance, "Really, Mama, I wish you had gone home. You could have taken Mr. FitzSimmons to escort you if you were afraid—though that is ridiculous, for I am sure you need no escort at all on such a rural road. But I have scarcely had an opportunity to get his lordship alone, and this would have been the perfect time. I declare, I could almost think you were trying to prevent Wycherly from making me an offer."

Aunt Lela opened her mouth to protest at this unfair accusation, then weakly closed it again. "Well, my love, I was quite willing to go—though to be sure, I can't think it exactly proper for you to be having tea with no more than a lone gentleman as your escort, however gentlemanly he may be! And besides," she added more strongly, "I've no wish to criticize you, my love, but it was you who insisted upon inviting poor Mr. FitzSimmons to come and stay at the same time as his lordship. You can hardly order him about as if he were just a footman."

"Good Lord, Mama, don't be so naive! I daresay he

knows himself I only invited him to make Wycherly jealous and bring him up to scratch," said Livia in annoyance, turning away from the mirror after a last pat to her golden curls. She cast a look of dislike at Sorrel and added with equal unfairness, "And *you* might have refrained from playing the helpless female and keeping him at your side all morning, when it was obvious he was longing to come with us!" she said venomously.

Sorrel's cheeks were hot, but no more than her aunt did she bother to protest this highly biased view of events. Instead she merely said stiffly, "You may assure his lordship for me that good manners do not require him to make such a sacrifice. In fact, I wish you would!"

Livia was in no way appeased, however. "Don't think I don't know what you're up to," she said unpleasantly. "If it weren't so pathetic it would be hilarious. You don't seriously think he's likely to be interested in you, with your die-away airs and dowdy dresses, do you, and all that talk of having been a heroine?"

"Livia!" exclaimed her mama, for once moved to expostulate.

But Livia merely shrugged. "Well, it is as well to get things clear between us, Mama. Besides, I wouldn't like Sorrel to misunderstand his lordship's attentions. If he has paid any attention to her, it is only out of pity."

"*Pity?*" repeated Sorrel sharply.

Livia looked pleased to have gotten to her for once. "Yes, of course. After all, you are a stranger here, and you have done everything you could to appeal to his chivalry, with your convenient accident, and that deceptively shy air of yours. It almost makes me laugh, cousin, for however sorry he may feel for you, he is scarcely likely to look twice at you as a woman. In fact, he told me once that you tended to fade into the woodwork."

Sorrel's cheeks were flushed with anger by then, but it was her aunt who again said sharply, looking worriedly between them, "Livia! You apologize at once. I won't have trouble between you, on top of everything else."

But Sorrel had herself well in hand again by then. So much for Mrs. Harris's suspicions, for it seemed clear that if the marquis had indeed been watching her, it was not out of admiration. "It's all right, Aunt," she said a little wearily. "It is, as my cousin says, well to have matters clear between us. You may rest easy, Livia. I have not the least desire to try and cut you out with his lordship, even if I could."

Livia looked not the least discomfited. "Good. It is as well to have things clear, as I said. And now I think we should go downstairs again, for the gentlemen will be waiting."

"One moment," said Sorrel unexpectedly. "Since we are being so delightfully frank, I have a question for you, cousin. Do you love him?"

Livia shrugged, and did not even bother to lie. "Don't be absurd. I like him very well, and meant from the beginning to have him, for I think it will exactly suit me to be a marchioness. But I don't mean to be in love with anybody, if you want the truth. It makes people foolish and sentimental, and I have too much ambition for that. In some ways it's even a shame it is not Mr. FitzSimmons with the title, for he is a much better dresser, and so very polished. Besides," she added with perhaps more frankness than she intended, "I know exactly where I stand with him. But then his lordship is the better-looking of the two, and I don't doubt we shall deal excellently together. Don't look so shocked, cousin. I don't mean that he hasn't fallen in love with me, for most men do. But if I am marrying him because he is rich and can give me the title I have always wanted, he is marrying me because I am beautiful and sought-after, and will make him an excellent hostess. We are neither of us under any illusions, you see."

"Yes, I do see," said Sorrel dryly. "I hope you will be very happy together."

Livia's beautiful eyes had narrowed, for she had clearly disliked Sorrel's tone. "We will be! And now I think we had better go down, for we have kept the gentlemen waiting long enough. And if you have any pride at all, my dear American cousin, you will see to it that his lordship doesn't feel obliged to ride beside you the whole way home. I doubt you realize what a fool you are making of yourself."

Having thus effectively silenced her mother and cousin, Livia turned and led the way downstairs again, and over tea laughed and chatted as if in the best of spirits.

Sorrel, for her part, said even less than usual. She was still fighting the hurt and anger Livia's careless words had invoked. She might know Livia's accusations were prompted by spite, but there had been just enough truth in them to make her cringe. And to vow that his lordship would have no further cause to either pity her or fear that she was unduly interested in him.

Chapter 12

Sorrel had thought the day had held all it could in the way of unpleasantness for her, but it seemed she was mistaken. When they reached home again at last, it was to find a fashionable tilbury pulled up before the door, and a quantity of baggage being unloaded.

Aunt Lela sat up with a jerk, and said in astonishment, "What the—?" But she was not left in suspense for long, for even as they drew up, a dapper figure strolled out of the house, in a driving coat boasting no fewer than a dozen capes, and a fashionable shallow set at a rakish angle on his well-oiled locks.

Aunt Lela closed her mouth with a snap, and muttered under her breath with a marked lack of wifely affection, "It's Walter! Drat and curse the man! I might have known he'd show up to put the finishing touches to everything else that's gone wrong already!"

Despite the miserable day she had just spent, Sorrel had to bite back a laugh, especially since her aunt spoke quite loudly enough for her third husband, whose arrival they had interrupted, to hear.

But Walter, as usual, was wholly impervious to snubs. He strolled down the steps, saying heartily, "Oh, there you are! Beginning to think the place was deserted. Hello, my dear! Been out on the toddle?"

Her aunt frowned even more portentously, and demanded bluntly, as she prepared to descend from the carriage, "What are you doing here?"

Walter's smile remained determinedly fixed in place.

"Why, I was in the neighborhood, don't you know, and thought I'd just take a look in." He saluted the wife of his bosom with a careless kiss on the cheek, and lowered his voice in what he fondly imagined to be a whisper. "I see I must congratulate you, my dear! So you brought Wycherly up to scratch after all? I must confess I never thought you'd do it, especially inviting him to such a tumbledown place as this! Lord, where have your wits gone! I took one look at it and almost drove off again, for it looks deuced uncomfortable, if you ask me. But it would seem to have done the trick. When's the wedding to be?"

Aunt Lela directed a glance of loathing at him. "Never, if you stick your oar in," she said fiercely. "But I might have known you'd show up to ruin everything."

"Now there you ain't using your head!" said her husband rather impatiently, his mask of bonhomie slipping slightly. "Which surprises me, for usually you're as shrewd as you can hold together, which I know to my cost," he added bitterly. "I assure you it's as much in my interest as yours to have Wycherly safely riveted to the Luscious Livia—though I don't envy him, poor chap! In fact, it's why I came, for I knew if I left it all up to you, you'd manage to throw a spanner in the works somehow. But I might have known my good intentions would be misinterpreted. You take pleasure in finding me in the wrong."

"If I do, it's because I know you too well," retorted her aunt grimly. "Well I know you've no thought in your head but feathering your own nest—usually at my expense! I suppose the truth is you're in debt again. But I warned you the last time that I wouldn't pay a penny more even if it meant rescuing you from the spunging house."

Sorrel feared every word of this was audible to the riding party that had drawn up behind them and were even now dismounting. But she was too resigned to the enmity between the couple to have any hope of silencing them, or even making them lower their voices.

But Walter glanced over his shoulder and said mockingly, "How charming, my dear. But at least I am well bred enough to know not to wash my dirty linen in public. D'you wish his lordship to hear every word of this interesting discussion? A fine impression that will be!" He then somewhat spoiled his effect by adding, "Besides, I've a scheme in my head that will set me up for life—and I will be demmed glad to be free of your purse strings, I can tell you!"

It seemed likely that the damage had already been done, but Sorrel unwillingly raised her voice to second Walter. "Pray, Aunt, he's right for once. You may quarrel with Walter to your heart's content later."

Aunt Lela reluctantly swallowed her spleen, though her eyes still glittered wrathfully, but Walter turned to greet the guests with unimpaired suavity. His stepdaughter he hailed with even less enthusiasm than he had his wife, and received for his pains a glare of dislike that would have cut through any less impenetrable armor. In fact, the only thing Sorrel knew to be to her aunt's third husband's credit was that for some reason he was wholly immune to Livia's attractions. But since it was likely that this unexpectedly clear vision sprang from the fact that he was by far too selfish himself to appreciate that quality in anyone else, she was easily able to refrain from admiring him for it. In fact he said frequently in her mother's hearing that his stepdaughter might be the most highly finished piece of nature to grace the *ton* within his memory, but his taste had never run to spoiled and temperamental beauties. Besides, he had no doubt that she would subject whatever poor unfortunate devil she at last succeeded in entrapping into marriage to a life of petticoat rule—especially if she held the purse strings, which seemed all-too likely.

Not surprisingly, Livia in turn was extremely contemptuous of him, and even more outspoken on the subject; and Sorrel had already discovered to her cost that when the two of them were living in the same household, life tended to be even more tempestuous than usual.

But at least even Aunt Lela could seldom find fault with Walter's appearance or his manners. Compared to the marquis, whose dress was at all times modest and extremely elegant, Sorrel thought Walter must always look ridiculous. But in the eyes of the world she knew he was counted a handsome figure, though drink and excess were beginning to have their inevitable effect. He was always dressed in the exaggerated style of a dandy, drove a flashy pair of bays, lost huge sums nightly at play, and seemed quite content to live off his wife's fortune without in the least feeling it incumbent upon himself to show her any respect in company. Indeed, he was too apt to deprecate her connection to trade among the more high-born of his cronies for Sorrel's liking, and having made his acquaintance shortly after coming to live with her aunt, she had been as relieved as her aunt was when he took himself off to stay with a convivial company of friends in the country.

In marrying for the third time a man some fifteen years younger than she was, and one whose fortune was so far beneath her own, Aunt Lela was the first to admit she had for once allowed her emotions to overcome her reason. Handsome, self-assured, born into the social set that had forever excluded her, he had seemed to promise the entrée to the *ton* that she had always sought, particularly in light of her aspirations for her beautiful daughter. But as she complained openly, it had all been nothing but a take-in. Mr. Walter Granville might have been *born* into the right set, as he was too fond of pointing out to her; but since that enviable achievement, she said frankly, he had seemed intent upon doing what he could to set up the backs of those whose opinions most mattered. From a ruinous career at Oxford, where he had been sent down for getting the daughter of a respectable publican into trouble, he had proceeded to become a young rake on the town, addicted to all the more ruinous forms of drink and gaming, and was now well confirmed in most forms of vice and excess.

All this she had only discovered after the wedding, of course. That he was extremely expensive as well disturbed her aunt less than the rest, for as she said frankly, she could afford it, and she had expected to pay down her blunt for the perceived advantages in such a connection. But what she had not bargained for was that having had the most desperate of his debts settled (for which he was not in the least grateful, and indeed had rapidly embarked upon a new round of dissipation in keeping with his suddenly improved financial position), not only did Walter show himself supremely indifferent to his new stepdaughter's social advancement, but had so ruined himself with the *ton* that he could not have helped her even had he wished to.

In fact, Aunt Lela said with her accustomed bluntness that it was the only time she could remember being fair diddled, for there was no denying that she had been completely taken in, which was not a thing that much happened to her. To a certain degree the name Granville had gained her a slight advantage, which the name of her latest husband, an exceedingly wealthy merchant, would not have done. And fortunately Livia's beauty had done the rest. But since a divorce would have caused the very scandal Aunt Lela was most determined should not mar her daughter's chances, she was forced to live with the results of her one major mistake.

That was a slight misstatement, for in general she did not live in the same house with him. Walter was generally to be found in Newmarket or Leicester or Brighton, or wherever the company was convivial and the stakes were the highest, for he was addicted to sport of all kinds. He was wholly uninterested in the sort of tame entertainments Aunt Lela had married him to gain entrée to. In London they now and then lived together, but they led completely separate lives, and in truth, once past his youthful peccadilloes, even Aunt Lela had to admit that Walter seemed largely uninterested in the fairer sex. She did not scruple to confide to her niece that she was sure he had a mistress in keeping somewhere that he was no doubt squandering her money on, but the latter fact, rather than inspiring her to jealousy, seemed merely to add to her indignation.

Sorrel personally felt that he was far too vain to waste his time on women at all. Certainly he squandered even more of her aunt's fortune on himself, for he was always extravagantly dressed, and was never without a new and expensive hack, or the latest racing curricle. Hence the expensive chestnut, bought at an exorbitant price and never ridden.

Now Aunt Lela cast a darkling look at the newcomer and said angrily, and unfortunately still quite audibly, "Lord! As if I did not have enough already to plague me!"

Sorrel glanced across unwittingly at the marquis, whose presence she had taken care to ignore the whole afternoon, and for one moment their eyes met, in perfect comprehension. Then Sorrel hastily and stonily looked away again, having no wish to share even that much with him.

But Walter, as usual, was wholly unfazed, and blithely went to shake hands with his wife's guests, claiming an acquaintanceship with Mr. FitzSimmons, whom he knew slightly, and behaving toward the marquis with a fawning flattery that Sorrel greatly disliked.

For his part, the marquis was more restrained, saying merely, "How do you do? I fancy I have seen you once or twice in London."

Mr. Granville waved an airy hand. "Oh, aye," he said complacently, "I'm sure you may meet me anywhere. But I must confess I'm devilish glad to meet you! In fact, demmed glad I came, though I'll confess it was not something I was looking forward to—especially after I cast my eyes over the place! Looks to be falling apart, and in my opinion, there's nothing so tame as country-house-parties anyway. All picnics and charades, and polite tittle-tattle. Devilish dull, upon my word! In fact, I daresay you'll be glad enough of my arrival, for we can get up a game between us, now and then, to help pass the time, eh? Nothing could be better!"

Aunt Lela looked furious, and his lordship's eyes had begun to twinkle again, for Walter's friendly little games were well known to start at extremely ruinous stakes, and to last all night. But he said gravely, "I fear you are much above my touch, Mr. Granville. Besides, I could not, in all conscience, abandon such charming company."

"As to that," said Walter, with an unflattering glance at his impatient stepdaughter, "in my opinion you can have too much of a good thing. But aye, we'll talk of it later. As for being above your touch, that's a rich one, if even half of what I've heard is true. Stepped into Wycherly's shoes, didn't you? And what he was thinking of not to provide an heir of his own is more than I can guess. Ramshackle, it seems to me. In fact, it just goes to prove what I've always said, that you're either born with luck or you ain't. I mean, here you are, his heir for all those years, admittedly, but with never any guarantee he wouldn't one day take it into his head to get a son of his own, and cut you out of the succession. And with my luck that's just what would have happened. I'd find myself supplanted at the last minute by a bran-faced brat young enough to be my son, and with nothing to show for it but a passel of post-obit bonds which would have to be settled. But then I was always devilish unlucky."

Aunt Lela was looking outraged, but to his credit the marquis merely looked even more amused. "You're right, there is never any accounting for luck," he agreed. "But I believe my uncle was devoted to my aunt."

"The more fool he, then," said Mr. Granville even more frankly. "All I can say is, you must have breathed a sigh of relief when he at last stuck his spoon in the wall, leaving the whole to you, along with the title. I hear he cut up extremely rich, too. As I said, some men have all the luck."

"I am sure his lordship is wholly uninterested in your speculations on his affairs," said Aunt Lela coldly. "In the meantime, you are keeping us standing when we have had an exhausting day already. Pray come in, my lord. I can't think what my husband can be thinking of to keep you hanging about outside."

She shepherded her guests indoors, and there the party thankfully split up, Walter promising to see them all at dinner, before wandering off to oversee his unpacking.

"And I'll wager a groat against a handsaw that he's in debt again," fumed Aunt Lela, steaming up the stairs to her own bedchamber with her daughter and Sorrel in tow. "As if things were not bad enough already. And to have to introduce him to his lordship at this juncture, with everything still undecided, is the outside of enough, and would put anyone to the blush! Lord knows his mission in life seems to be to make my life miserable, and why I ever came to marry him is more than I can tell you now. But at the very least I thought I could rely upon him to be busy with his ruinous friends, which is one of the reasons I settled upon it to come here, for well I knew how he feels about country house parties—or at least, any that don't include those precious cronies of his, playing whist at pound points and drinking themselves into a stupor every night, and for all I know including the sort of brazen-faced hussies which are the only sort to consort with the likes of them, for I'm sure any decent woman would be disgusted. But if he thinks to put a spoke in my plans and embarrass me with his lordship, he's mistaken, for I'm willing to put up with a lot to avoid a scandal—which you may be sure is what he's counting on!—but not that."

When exercised, as she was now, her voice was a carrying one, and Sorrel cast an anxious glance at the walls, hoping they were thicker than she supposed. "Dearest Aunt, hush! It is bad enough without letting his lordship hear you! As for the marquis, I feel sure he—he has already taken Walter's measure."

"Aye, I'll make no doubt he has—though it's small comfort to me to be obliged to introduce such a creature as my husband," said her aunt grimly.

"Then you shouldn't have married him," put in Livia, coldly furious, "as I told you at the time. Well, all I can say is that he must be got rid of, Mama, and at once! I don't care if you have to bribe him, or have him kidnapped. I won't have him spoiling my chances with Wycherly."

"Well, I daresay I would do even that, if I thought it would answer," responded her mama frankly. "Only ten to one I could not find anyone willing to kidnap him here, though I make no doubt in London I could find someone to murder him for me for a pittance. Not that I would go so far, you understand, though I'll confess I have more than once been tempted. But, my love, you cannot have thought it out completely, for now that the wretched creature is here, it would seem even more embarrassing if he were to disappear just as suddenly, and we were obliged to try and explain it to his lordship."

"Good God, ma'am, Wycherly don't care what becomes of Walter. You may safely leave that to me. But have him spoiling everything I will not, if I have to murder him myself."

"No, no, my love, I am sure I will think of something."

Livia cast her a contemptuous glance. "Make sure you do. I have made up my mind to bring his lordship up to scratch before this visit is over, and you may be sure nothing is going to be allowed to stand in my way, certainly not Walter! If you cannot control your own husband, he shall have to be got rid of, for I won't have him offending Wycherly and ruining everything."

"No, my love," said her mama unhappily. "Though

how I am to get rid of him is more than I can guess, now that he's here."

"Buy him off, if you have to!" said Livia crudely. She cast another slightly narrowed glance at Sorrel, who had remained silent during the last part of this discussion, and added, as if deliberately, "I intend to be the Marchioness of Wycherly by the time the year is out. And I can only repeat that nothing or *no one* is going to be allowed to stand in my way."

Chapter 13

But for once Aunt Lela's forebodings seemed un-
founded. Walter was on his best behavior, and even
she had to reluctantly admit that it took some of the pressure off her to have a host to help entertain the gentlemen.

If he did not succeed in inveigling them into an expensive and lengthy card game (at least to Aunt Lela's
knowledge), or in getting the male members of the party
to take a bolt to some nearby village where a prizefight
was being held, he did take the gentlemen out for a day's
shooting, and accompanied the entire party when they
drove into Stratford to visit the home of the famous
Bard.

Here, too, he said frankly he'd no notion why anyone
would drive out of their way to gawk at a tumble-down
ruin, and go into raptures over a book with a lot of silly
signatures of famous people in it who were gudgeons
enough to have done the same.

Sorrel saw the marquis's amusement at this opinion,
but it seemed clear that Livia privately agreed with her
stepfather for once. She soon found an excuse to draw
Wycherly away from the house and out into the gardens,
by complaining of the heat inside. And she followed up
on this advantage by afterward strolling with both of her
suitors down to the river, where it was found they could
hire a boat and go out and feed the swans.

Sorrel politely declined to accompany the boating
party, and while both her aunt and stepuncle recruited

their strength by dozing in rare accord side by side in the shade, she retraced her steps to the Bard's birthplace. There she admired the few scant possessions still remaining in the house, and listened to the tales of the great Mr. Shakespeare (probably mostly apocryphal) told by the caretaker, a distant relation.

She lost track of the time, in fact, and returned to find the boating party already back, and Livia looking impatient and his lordship a trifle grim.

She had reason to suspect that he was still keeping a close eye on her, though she had been successful in eluding any further tête-à-têtes with him. Walter's coming had helped in that regard, at least, and she had taken care since the picnic always to remain in the company of her cousin or her aunt.

But it was Livia who said impatiently, "If you must go off on your own, cousin, I wish you would not keep the rest of us waiting. Pray let us go now. I have had quite enough of sightseeing for one morning."

Sorrel was thinking of that the next morning, as she arranged flowers in the ancient church next door. She suspected her cousin's increasing temper sprang from the fact that the marquis's visit was drawing to a close, and he had yet to make her an offer. He was invariably polite and charming and paid Livia elaborate compliments, as did Mr. FitzSimmons. But no amount of angling on Livia's part had succeeded in forcing him into making a declaration.

Thinking of the things he had revealed to her about his sudden accession to the title, Sorrel wondered if he was deliberately holding out, refusing to give in to such obvious stratagems. That he intended ultimately to wed her seemed clear. But perhaps he had no intention of allowing Livia to force him into making her an offer before he was ready to make one.

If so, she could scarcely blame him, but it was making life miserable for the rest of them. Livia was certainly growing impatient, and more and more suspicious of her

American cousin. All in all, it would be a relief when the betrothal was announced, for it seemed that none of them would have any peace until it was.

Sorrel deliberately closed her mind to the fact that the news of his engagement to her cousin would be more of a blow than she wanted to admit. It seemed it was inevitable, and she did not fool herself into thinking his unusual attitude toward her meant anything. But she knew him well enough by then to hate to see him caught in her cousin's toils.

That day Livia had gone out for a drive with both of her suitors, each laughingly vying with the other for the privilege of handing her into his lordship's curricle. From the vantage point of her bedchamber window Sorrel had seen them set off, and since Livia was always at her best when at the center of attention, she had been in excellent spirits. For her part, Sorrel had taken good care that none of them should see her and had drawn back at once, not wanting to spoil the moment or seem to be spying on them.

But at least it gave her a free afternoon. Thinking herself safe, she took the opportunity to visit her unknown grandparents' graves, then took her flowers in to arrange them on the altar.

She had had her tea with the vicar's wife some days before, and had found her a delightful woman. They had talked of the twins when they were girls, of what Mrs. Harris could remember of Sorrel's own grandparents, whom of course she had never met, and of Sorrel's life in America. Sorrel could only be grateful that the conversation did not once veer onto more dangerous grounds.

Mrs. Harris was inclined to view the freedom Sorrel enjoyed in America with wonder, and said several times, "Well, well! Who'd have thought it? It must indeed be a fine country."

They had subsequently parted on the best of terms, and Sorrel was thinking back to that visit with some pleasure when she heard footsteps on the stone floor behind her.

At first she thought it must be the vicar, or even his wife, and did not pay much attention. But then a voice she knew too well said in approval, "Very pretty. It seems there is no end to your accomplishments, Miss Kent."

She was unnaturally startled, and her heart betrayed her by quickening ridiculously. She wheeled around and could not quite prevent herself from saying revealingly, "But I thought you—"

"Ah, then that was you at the window," he said in amusement. "I thought it was. I decided after all not to go, for my curricle was not built for three. And it seems we have had little opportunity to have any more private chats, you and I, Miss Kent."

Before she could react in alarm to that likely threat, he went on conversationally, "In fact, I saw you earlier putting flowers on your grandparents' graves. It must be odd to find so many roots here, in this country, that you didn't know about."

"It is not in the least odd," she said a little sharply, turning back to her task with determination. "I know where my roots are, and they are all in America."

He smiled, as if amused by her prickliness. "So you keep telling me. And yet surely these are equally your roots? Your mother was born here, and you have now met relations you never knew, and people who knew your mother, and now you are seeing things perhaps a little differently."

When she made no answer, somewhat surprised at his acuity, he went on ruefully, "I must confess I know a little what that is like, as a matter of fact. I spent many years abroad, and when I came back to England, it was almost like a foreign country to me."

She frowned at the unexpected revelation, and blurted out before she could prevent herself, "Is that why you seem to belong everywhere and nowhere?"

He looked startled, but unoffended. "I don't know. Do I?"

She was sorry she had started it, but said more slowly, "Yes, you do. Your manners are always easy and excellent, and you have the knack of seeming to fit in anywhere. And yet there is a part of you that seems completely unreachable."

"If so, we have that in common, for I could say the same of you," he pointed out. "I have noticed you, too, have a habit of withdrawing into the woodwork, Miss Sorrel Kent, and I am seldom sure what you are thinking. Perhaps we are more alike than you are willing to acknowledge."

She turned abruptly away and finished her flowers, thinking that Livia had been right in her unkind words. She wondered if he knew how unflattering his estimation of her was. His withdrawing was merely a matter of keeping a part of himself intact, while showing only the charming surface to the world. Hers went far deeper than that and was not something anyone who had been accepted and sure of himself all his life was in the least likely to be able to understand.

After a moment the marquis said curiously, "Why did you come to England, Miss Kent?"

"To meet my aunt and cousin, of course and to——" Then she broke off, for perhaps his unexpected honesty deserved the same from her. "Perhaps I did come in search of my roots," she conceded reluctantly. "I thought I was all American. And I am, of course. Yet meeting my aunt, and coming to this village where my mother grew up, shows me that I have roots here, too. My mother used to speak of this church, you know. I knew what it looked like before ever I saw it. Come here."

She had finished the flowers, and she surprised even herself a little by leading him to a small sanctuary in the south corner, instead of trying to run away. "This is the tomb of Sir Baptist Hicks. He built Campden House, you know. Mama used to tell me of him when I was little, and of his granddaughter, Lady Penelope Noel, who died as a result of pricking her finger while sewing with colored silks. As a child I used to imagine so tragic a death, and how her parents must have grieved for her. I must confess I feel more grief here, however absurdly, than I did at my own grandparents' graves.

He admired the life-size effigy of a very stiff Lord and Lady Campden lying under a huge canopy, and the much smaller one to the Lady Penelope. "I can see how it might have appealed to your imagination. How odd it must be to think of generations looking at our monuments, years from now. Not that I mean to put up such a monument to myself, I must confess. It seems a great deal too—pompous, if nothing else. But perhaps I saw too many deaths in wartime to believe spirits linger or the effects of death can be soothed by the putting up of an expensive monument."

Then something must have crossed her face, for he said quickly, "I'm sorry. That was clumsy of me."

She took a breath. "No. It is almost a year now. And like you, I could not find—solace—in cold marble."

He took another look at her face, and said abruptly, "With all apologies to Sir Baptist and his family, I always find tombs oppressive. If you are finished with your flowers let us go outside again."

She knew she should find some excuse to leave him— had delayed too long in fact—but she allowed herself to be escorted outside, for she had suddenly had too much of the church, too. After a moment, he said, "Forgive me, but you said your fiancé—died in your arms, and I understand from your aunt that you went to nurse the wounded. I don't mean to be presumptuous, but sometimes it helps to talk of it, you know."

She doubted it, especially to such an audience. "But then you of all people must know that is nothing to boast of. One does—what one has to do, and I hope I may never experience such horror again. But only those who have lived through it can possibly understand that."

He had stopped walking for some reason, and she found herself following suit. Now he turned to face her and said seriously, "No. Good God, no. People will persist in asking me to recount my adventures of war to them. My adventures! They mean, of course, some amusing anecdote, and certainly there were plenty of those. But they have no conception of what war really means, of course."

She shuddered involuntarily. "No. Or that it is scarcely a fit topic for light after-dinner conversation."

"As I said, I begin to think we have a great deal more in common than you would like to admit, Miss Kent," he said. "I certainly never expected to find a woman who understood that. Perhaps that is what you meant when you said earlier that I was not—wholly here. You must know that once having experienced those—horrors, it is somehow difficult to return to normal life and see importance in the cut of one's coat or the latest *on-dit*. I sometimes do feel, as you say, that I drift around, being pleasant and polite, while the real me is still somewhere else, and I'm no longer even sure where."

She could not prevent herself from looking up into his face, surprise and something else in her eyes, for if he had never thought to find a woman who understood that, she certainly had never thought to hear such words from so fashionable a man, or that he could indeed understand what she herself had only partially understood in herself. "Yes," she said unwillingly. "That is what it's like. I keep telling myself I should be glad to be back in a safe, sane world again. I am glad. And yet, it all seems a little unreal to me. I keep remembering—"

"Don't," he said quickly. "I didn't mean to bring such horrors back again. But forgive me. I can't help wondering why your family didn't send you to England then, for safety?"

She smiled a little sarcastically at that. "You forget, the British had the Chesapeake blockaded for most of the war. Besides, I wouldn't have gone, for nurses were needed desperately. I may not know how to flirt behind a fan in a ballroom, but I am a good nurse. I was at our plantation when they landed troops near St. Michael's, and took Kent Island. I was in Annapolis the night they burned Washington to the ground and we all thought we would be next. And I was there to nurse the wounded at Fort McHenry. I may not have been a soldier myself, but there is little you can teach me of war."

"And I was forgetting that we were the enemy," he said with what sounded surprisingly like bitterness. "I have set myself a larger task than I knew."

Since she couldn't guess what he meant by that, and was not about to ask, she said truthfully, "There were certainly times when, like everyone else, I hated and feared the British."

"A much larger task! Is that why you dislike me and refuse to trust me?"

She stiffened instinctively, not wanting to be reminded of all the reasons she had for avoiding his company. "I don't dislike you," she said reluctantly.

"Well that is something, I suppose," he said ruefully. "No, don't poker up! I am well aware that for some reason you don't trust me. Whether that is because of the recent war between our countries, or merely your prejudice against my title, I have no idea. But I am generally accounted a good man in a fight, you know. Cannot you bring yourself to let me help you?"

She blushed hotly, and could have cursed the betraying sign. His raillery she could easily resist, but it was much harder to resist so gentle a tone, and the warm smile that went with it. In fact it would be fatally easy to give in to the faint tenderness she seemed to find in his manner, for in truth she was beginning to think him a man who could be trusted.

But then what? she derided herself. Did she really think to play the weak-willed woman and cast all her troubles at his feet, expecting him to pick them up? He had broad enough shoulders for even that, if the truth be acknowledged. But she was no fair maid to his knight errant. And besides, he was about to marry her cousin. "Why should I?" she demanded truthfully.

He shrugged. "That is indeed the question," he agreed. "And if you don't yet know the answer to that, then I'm afraid I can't help you. All I can say is that for an intelligent woman, Miss Kent, you are amazingly blind sometimes."

There seemed to be no reply she could make to that, and so she made none. After a moment, as if accepting defeat, he sighed and determinedly tucked one of her unresponsive hands in his arm and started walking again, remarking conversationally, "And I can see I have had my answer. Never mind. Only I hope you have not forgotten my earlier promise to you, for I still intend to keep it. You shall confide in me sooner or later, and trust me too, Miss Sorrel Kent of America."

He then blithely changed the subject and began to walk again, as if the previous scene had not happened. "You know, it is really a very fine old house," he said as they left the church grounds and began to stroll toward the Lodge gates of Campden House. "It is a shame it has been allowed to fall into such disrepair. I can see why your aunt admired it so much when she was a girl."

She was grateful for the change of topic, and so said with perhaps more enthusiasm than she might ordinarily have revealed, "I confess I have quite lost my heart to it. My mama used to speak of it, so I felt as if I knew it already. When Aunt Lela found out it was available for lease she was a little bemused, I think, for she and my mama used to dream of living here when they were girls. Then it was the finest house in the neighborhood, and wholly beyond their reach, or so they thought."

"Yes, I have heard stories of their remarkable success. I do not know your mama, of course, but I must confess I find your aunt a constant delight."

She looked at him suspiciously, suspecting some irony in his tone, but could detect none in his face. But that at least served to remind her of reality, and she subtly withdrew her arm, pretending to wish to dislodge a stone in her sandal.

He patiently waited until she finished this operation, and then they began to stroll again. "Yes," she said with determined brightness. "You have only to look at my cousin to understand what they must have looked like."

He merely smiled. "Perhaps your aunt will end by purchasing this house. Has she discussed it?"

Sorrel was again grateful for the change of subject. "No, for my cousin dislikes the country." That sounded churlish, so she went on quickly, "It almost burned down once, during your Civil War, you know. You can tell by the redness of the stone the parts of the house that were involved in the fire, for I am told that Cotswold stone always turns red when it is heated."

He glanced at her in unmistakable amusement. "Very interesting."

She plowed on a little desperately, determined to keep the conversation on a neutral topic. "Is your own home very much grander? I must confess we don't tend to such—mansions at home. Perhaps it is against our democratic principles, but I find I do not care for some of the huge palaces my aunt has pointed out to me. I prefer something cozier like this, despite its shabbiness."

He smiled a little ruefully. "My own home—the one I grew up in—was not much bigger. Keep in mind my father was but a younger son. My home now is—very much grander and a little impersonal. You would not find it in the least cozy, I'm afraid. I confess I spend as little time in it as possible. But then I have been used, in the last years, to consider myself in the lap of luxury if I had a roof over my head that didn't leak, and boasted a fireplace and not a mere hole in the ceiling to allow the smoke to escape. Which reminds me."

But what that reminded him of she was never to discover. They had reached the house by then, and continued to walk toward the porch. Afterward Sorrel remembered being grateful that her cousin was indeed away and could not see them walking together. But just as they reached the house there was a loud scraping sound from above.

Sorrel looked up, startled. The next moment the marquis had thrust her bodily out of the way, just as something crashed to the ground with a sound like an explosion and shattered there, exactly on the spot where she had been standing.

Chapter 14

Under the impetus of that thrust, Sorrel stumbled and fell heavily to the gravel drive, painfully grazing her hands and knees through the thin stuff of her gown. For a moment she scarcely took in what had happened. Then the marquis was there, picking her up bodily and exclaiming, "Sorrel! Good God, are you all right?"

"Yes," she said breathlessly. "What on earth happened?" She scarcely noticed his use of her first name and was equally unaware that her hands were scraped and bleeding, her gown was dusty, and there was a streak of dirt on one cheek.

But he noticed all of those details. "What happened," he said grimly, "is that one of the chimneys nearly fell on you. Now tell me, you stubborn little idiot, that it is all my imagination and no one wishes to kill you. If I had not been here, they almost certainly would have succeeded this time."

She looked around with gathering horror, not wanting to believe him, but unable to argue with his assumptions. One of the decorative Elizabethan chimneys that she had so much admired had indeed fallen and all but disintegrated under the impact. Had she been standing under it she would almost certainly have been badly injured or even killed. "I don't—the chimneys are old, and the house is in a state of disrepair," she said weakly, beginning belatedly to shake. "Aunt Lela is always complaining of it."

He, too, seemed thrown out of his habitual good temper, for he said in quick exasperation, "God give me patience! What does it take to get through to you? Don't you think you are taking your role as phlegmatic American a little too far?"

Then something in her shattered state got through to him, and he swore under his breath, then said more gently, "I'm sorry! You are shaken all to pieces and it is little wonder. I will admit my nerves are none too steady, for I thought sure you must be killed. My dear, don't look like that!"

She had no idea how she looked, and indeed despised herself for her show of weakness. She thought it was the sound of the exploding chimney that had affected her more than anything, for it sounded too uncomfortably like the sound of cannon, which she had hoped never to hear again. But whatever it was, she found her teeth had begun to chatter as if she were suffering from the cold, even though it was an extremely warm June day. "It is n-nothing!" she tried to say. "I will be b-better s-shortly."

But he seemed not to believe her reassurances, for his hands tightened painfully on her grazed ones, and he said with an odd kind of suppressed violence, "Hell and the devil confound it! It is at least good to know that even the redoubtable Miss Kent is capable of so human a reaction. But let me get you inside to your aunt."

But that at least got through to her, for the last thing she wished was for her aunt to know of this latest accident—or for his lordship to begin to question her aunt directly. Indeed, she badly needed time to think; but at the moment her brain seemed incapable of rational thought. She had not thought she would fall apart so much at what, after all, was no more than a near-disaster. Thanks to his lordship's quick thinking and even quicker reactions, she was alive and well and mostly unharmed. It was more than time that she pulled herself together.

"N-no!" she said more vehemently than she intended. "D-don't be ridiculous. I will be better p-presently. It is n-nothing. Just the noise. It's silly, I know, but for a moment I thought it was c-cannon fire."

He took another look at her white face and huge eyes, and abruptly pulled her into his arms, holding her tightly and stroking her tumbled hair back as if she had been a little girl again, in need of comfort, saying matter-of-factly, "I know. It's not silly. I still dream I am under attack sometimes."

She was grateful for his kindness, but she should pull away before it was too late. Instead, she shivered involuntarily, and his arms tightened still more. "So this is what it takes to shake your monumental calm!" he murmured into her hair, sounding breathless himself for some reason, and half amused again. "I don't mean to frighten you any more than necessary—and I am enjoying this temporary weakness—but perhaps now you will take me more seriously, my dear. No, no! Don't try to pull away. If you are not upset, my nerves are shot to hell, and I need some proof that you are still whole and in one piece. When I looked up and saw that chimney falling straight toward you, I lost a good year of my life from fright, I'm sure."

But despite his words—or perhaps because of them—after the first moment of giving in to the real comfort his arms provided, she knew she was finding it far too tempting to remain there and give way completely to the despised weakness within her. She felt safe there in a way she had not since indeed she had been a little child in her father's arms. But that was even more dangerous than the fallen chimney had been; and she no longer knew whether her breathlessness sprang from her near death or the feel of his arms about her.

She made herself pull away, and he released her a little, as if reluctantly, to look down at her from his superior height. She noticed for the first time that his coat was covered in a fine dust, and there was a rent in one elegant sleeve. "I should have known it would not be long before you began busily reerecting all your defenses again," he said ruefully. "You will soon be completely back in your shell, won't you, and I will have trouble imagining that this momentary softening ever occurred."

She feared she was not so successful at rebuilding her defenses as he imagined, but she said abruptly, "Let me go. I am all right now."

"Ah, yes, I can see you are almost yourself again. The independent Miss Kent: calm, a little condescending, and always aloof. I congratulate you on your speedy recovery, for my pulse has not yet ceased hammering, I must confess."

She could not believe he was talking of her. "Condescending? Are you mad?"

"Not in the least. Don't forget, I have observed you for almost a week now. You sit there in your corner, saying very little, and all the time observing the rest of us and the foolish things we get up to. But your eyes betray you, did you know? They are very beautiful and very expressive, and they are busily weighing and measuring and finding us all lamentably wanting."

Now she knew he must be mad—or else as overcome by the near accident as he claimed. "Is that meant as some kind of a joke?"

She would have pulled away completely then, but he would not let her go. She began to realize for the first time that despite his former gentleness, and his present mocking attitude, he was angry for some reason, though she could not begin to guess why.

"Not in the least. I might have been willing to dismiss you at your own evaluation that first day, had you not made the mistake of smiling at me. Did you know you look a different person when you smile? Even Fitz noticed it, and he seldom sees anything beyond his own nose. But you don't make that mistake too often, of course. I have scarcely seen you smile since. You are much too busy keeping people at a distance, building stone upon stone of that wall you set between yourself and the world. And safely behind it, you sit quietly thinking your own thoughts and playing second and even third fiddle to that—to your cousin, and freezing with a glance anyone who dares to try and get too close."

She was shaken to her very soul and almost as angry as he by that time. "I d-don't! It's not true."

"Isn't it, Miss Kent?" He was relentless. "Why else do you sit there, content to remain in the background when you are at least your cousin's equal in wit and breeding; and take your cousin's gibes without ever standing up for yourself? I know you to be a woman of spirit, don't forget. You seem to have little enough trouble standing up to me, for instance. And yet you might almost be a different girl in her presence. Why is that?"

"You forget," she said bitterly, "I am not quite my cousin's equal in—everything!"

There was a quick understanding in his face that she shrank from. "Ah! Is that what all this is about? Did you really believe all men were so easily bemused by mere physical beauty?"

"Most are." But she had revealed too much already, and so said quickly, desperately, "Look, perhaps you mean to be kind. But I—"

He gave a strangled laugh. "Kind? On the contrary, I am trying to knock some sense into you. But at least I begin to understand you, I think. You have played second fiddle to your beautiful mother, and now your cousin, until you seem to lack all the instincts of a normal and beautiful young girl. Did it never occur to you that men might find you attractive for yourself? What of this William? Your fiancé?"

She must stop this now. She said stiffly, "I don't want to talk of it. Please, this has gone far enough."

"On the contrary, I don't think it's gone nearly far enough. But I am indeed beginning to see," he said slowly. "I wondered, from what I knew of you, that you had ever relaxed your guard enough to become engaged."

She feared he had guessed nearly all of it now, and pride held her head up as she demanded defiantly, "Why don't you just say it? Like everyone else, you suspect William only became engaged to me because he was half in love with my mother."

"Oh, my dear," he said. "If he did, he was a fool, and wholly unworthy of you."

"Do you think I want your *pity*?"

""Pity?" He almost laughed again. "For an intelligent woman, you are even blinder than I had thought, my dear Sorrel. And my position is even more damnably awkward than I had already realized. It should be a lesson to me not to go off half-cocked, in future, out of boredom and feeling at loose ends, and general self-pity. But I can't have you continuing with so odd a misapprehension. Your cousin is indeed very beautiful, and I have no doubt your mother is as well. I also have no doubt that the majority of the men you know are fools. And yet, there are . . . those . . . who have the sense to appreciate your value."

"Oh, they appreciate my value all right. As nurse, big sister, confidante. Sensible Sorrel, whom everyone can rely on and who fades into the wall paper, as you said." She did not know why she was saying all this, for she had never done so before.

His hands tightened almost painfully on hers. "No, I can't let you go on thinking such things about yourself," he said. And abruptly, before she could begin to guess at what he would be at, he bent his head and pressed his lips to each tender palm.

She gave a strangled cry and tried to snatch her hands away. He raised his eyes swiftly and for a long moment their gazes locked, hers almost wild with panic and a truth she did not want to acknowledge.

For a moment longer she could hear her own blood rushing through her ears, and she could find nothing to say. She ought to pull away, leave before it was too late. But she knew it was already far too late, and whatever she did from now on would not change that.

Then he was kissing her, the beautifully shaped mouth suddenly shockingly on hers, giving her no chance to evade him. It was no gentle or respectful salute, as William had now and then given her. His lips were demanding, and though at first she fought against him, a muffled protest locked deep in her throat, he would not let her escape that easily. His hand had gone to the back of her head and he held her with shocking ease, molding her lips to fit his own as if he owned her, and making a mockery of her strength and vaunted independence.

Still she tried to fight him, though she knew with sick shame that she was losing her will. But even as she ceased to struggle, his lips changed, growing gentler, and beginning to coax rather than demand.

But it seemed she little understood the matter, as he must be very well aware of. It was only gradually that it began to occur to her that he was deliberately using her own weakness to defeat her. Still, even knowing it, and against every measure of her will she closed her eyes and gave way with a suddenness that must have surprised him.

If so, he did not reveal it. In triumph he gathered her closer and deepened the kiss again. His lips demanded a response from her, and they were sweet. Almost unbearably sweet. He made her feel absurdly small and helpless and—yes, beautiful, in a way she had never felt before.

Her own lips opened seemingly of their own volition beneath his, and she found herself kissing him back with a hunger that frightened her. Her arms, too, seemed to have a mind of their own, for they went instinctively around his neck to strain herself closer to him. And still she could not get close enough. She had never dreamed it could be this way between a man and a woman.

She felt the reaction in him instantly, and reveled in her power. Everything was a new sensation, and the best of it was that he was kissing her—not her mother—not her cousin. And kissing her as if he would never let her go, and had been waiting for this moment all of his life.

Chapter 15

Then, from one second to the next, her own thoughts acted like a brake on her mind, setting up the familiar, mocking refrain. He felt pity for her, that was all. Besides, how could she ever hope to compete with her beautiful cousin?

She became, in an unwanted instant, not the beautiful desirable creature of her fantasy, but merely herself, with all her awkward inadequacies and defenses. And she was kissing, in full view of the house and anyone who chanced to look out a window, a man who was handsome and titled, and of a different country; and, most important of all, who was all but betrothed to her beautiful cousin Livia.

He naturally felt the change in her, and at last lifted his head, though he did not immediately let her go. The hot light remained for a moment longer in his eyes, and for her own part she feared she was breathless, and flushed, and all too betrayingly weak.

For a moment longer they stared at each other, his own eyes narrowing, for she could not disguise the horror and recognition in her face. Then she pulled herself almost violently out of his arms. "No! Oh, let me go! *I can't!*"

He checked, the frown deepening between his brows and a sudden, almost wary expression on his own face. "Very well, but you don't have to sound so panicked. I will beg your pardon if you wish. I shouldn't have kissed you. But I must confess that I'm not in the least sorry that I did, and I will do it again at the first opportunity."

But she had turned away to bury her face in her hands in bitter shame and horror at her own actions. "Oh, God, what have I done? How could I?"

His brows rose a little, and some of the humor returned to his eyes. "It does complicate matters a little, I confess," he conceded ruefully. "But you needn't act so surprised, for it has been building between us since that first day. Besides, I would give much to know exactly why you are so horrified. Is it because it is too soon after your fiancé's death, or because we are former enemies; or merely because I am supposed to be one of your cousin's suitors?"

"All of those! None! Oh, do not let us talk of it. I am deeply ashamed. But it meant nothing."

"Console yourself with that thought if you can," he informed her dryly. "But we both know it is a lie."

"No! It can mean no more than that. If I thought it did I would go back to America tomorrow!" she cried wildly.

That checked him again for a moment. "I—see. And yet you still have not answered my question. Is it because it is too soon after your fiancé's death? Or because of your cousin? Because if so, I think—"

But she had in some measure regained her composure, and had turned back to him to say shakenly, "I'm sorry. I must be more shaken than I thought. Please, I beg you not to say any more. William—my cousin—our differing stations and beliefs. It is impossible. Please—I must go—! Do not try to come with me."

Her voice broke and she ignobly fled from him, without looking back to see if he followed, or if indeed their encounter had been observed by prying eyes from the house. She had long since completely forgotten the fallen chimney and her near disastrous accident.

She had remembered it by the time she regained her room, however. She should be concerned, frightened even. But a possible blackmailer stood little chance against her present turmoil.

Still, she made herself concentrate on it, to keep her mind off the last half hour. For she could no longer deny, even to herself, that she was in considerable danger. The first, the cutting of her girth, had not frightened her particularly, since it was the merest chance that she had been injured even as much as she was. She could not see how the accident could have been meant to be fatal, nor could her common sense discover a reason why it should have been.

No, the intent had seemed to be merely to frighten her aunt into paying over so large a sum. But this second incident was far more alarming. Had Wycherly not been there—but it did no good to think of that.

Nor with the best will in the world, could even she believe it was no more than a coincidence. The house was not in the best of repair, admittedly; but for the chimney piece to fall at that precise moment argued that it had been deliberately toppled. That she was not even now lying dead or seriously wounded was due to his lordship's unexpected presence (for he had supposed to be off driving with Livia) and his quick reflexes.

Unless—? Her brows drew together in an unconscious frown as a new thought struck her. Perhaps the very fact of the marquis's being there had been part of the plan. That was more reassuring, certainly, for the fatal turn the extortion attempt seemed to have taken had shaken her badly. But perhaps she was still right, and her actual death or serious harm had never been intended.

It was impossible to tell, especially in her present state. At the moment her brain did not seem to be working as logically as it should; and until she had thought it out more carefully she had no intention of informing her aunt of what had happened. That would merely alarm her and drive her into paying the demanded amount, which Sorrel was still opposed to. She only hoped she could rely upon the marquis to do the same.

That brought back what she was so desperately trying to forget, for she was well aware that it was not the near-accident that had so shaken her, and caused her, even now, to blush hotly whenever she thought of it.

That she had committed the supreme folly of falling in love with the Marquis of Wycherly was no longer to be denied. That was a bitter enough pill to swallow. But despite his kissing her so unexpectedly, it was clear he in turn felt nothing for her but pity. Why should he? However much she might search her heart—or her mirror—she could find only one answer to that. He, with the whole world at his feet, would be a fool to prefer her to her beautiful cousin.

No doubt he had meant to be kind. *Kind!* That was an even more bitter pill. But then she knew well that he was kind; and unexpectedly compassionate. And no doubt the awkward and shy cousin of the girl he meant to marry was a fitting object for his pity.

If that thought was almost too painful to be borne, it was yet the safest, after all. For even if, by some miracle, he had returned her affection, she had long realized she could not serve her aunt such a trick. She owed no particular allegiance or affection to her cousin, whom she cordially disliked. But her aunt had been unexpectedly kind to her, and she had grown genuinely fond of her in turn. To use that kindness to rob her of the thing she wanted above all else would be unforgivable.

But then, if Sorrel had come to think her beautiful cousin the last wife the marquis needed, and that he deserved much more than a shallow, vain, and opportunistic woman, however lovely; she doubted if most of the world would agree with her. She knew too well how mesmerized men could be by a pretty face, and how little they seemed to care whether strength of character or wits accompanied it. Very likely his lordship would wed the lovely Livia and never regret his choice, willingly trading what she saw as a true partnership of the mind and spirit for the more worldly advantage of inspiring the envy and admiration of all his friends.

She could not quite resist wasting a moment or two on a beatific dream. But she was too practical to indulge in such daydreams for long; and even her fantasy soon showed her how impossible it was. Not only her cousin, but too much else lay between them: country, beliefs, their very way of life. He was a titled Englishman, she an American who did not believe in titles. He had estates and responsibilities here, and she could not see herself giving up her own country to settle permanently in England. Besides, she had only to try to envision herself as a marchioness to realize how absurd it was. His life was social, and she was at her worst in a crowded ballroom or making polite conversation to strangers. Livia would indeed make him a better wife in that respect.

Her bruised heart insisted upon whispering foolishly that however at home in a ballroom she might be, Livia would not understand his need to be appreciated for himself, not his title. Or, once his ring was on her finger and his title hers, would she bother overmuch with sharing his interests or concerning herself with his well-being. She was quite amazingly selfish, and thought no further than of his exalted status and his material possessions. But then few men, looking into her huge blue eyes and basking in the glow of her flirtatious smile, would be inclined to consider such matters or think them of much importance at all. Sorrel had had a lifetime in which to adjust to that fact.

At least to Sorrel's relief, word of the latest accident seemed not to have spread. The fallen chimney stone was certainly much talked of, but no one seemed to guess at how close it had come to proving fatal, and even Aunt Lela merely complained of it during dinner that night, seeming to find it all of a piece with the other things that had gone wrong with the lease.

But on that topic she waxed indignant during most of

dinner, while Sorrel strove not to meet his lordship's eyes and kept her own attention firmly on her plate. Walter, too, seemed little interested in the topic. But Sorrel was relieved when Livia, never one to enjoy a conversation not centered about herself, grew impatient, and at last put an end to it. "Well, if you will hire a house that is all but falling apart, Mama, what can you expect? Remember, I was against the scheme from the beginning. In fact, I am of the opinion that when our guests leave, we should do likewise, and spend the rest of the summer in some civilized place such as Brighton, where there is at least something to do, and shops and balls and parties to relieve the boredom."

Aunt Lela blinked, and said weakly, "Well, my love, but don't forget I have let the house for the entire summer. Not that that would signify, of course. But I am sure you have not been bored with his lordship and Mr. FitzSimmons here. Didn't you have a nice drive this afternoon?"

Livia tossed her head and shot a challenging glance at his lordship through her golden lashes. "Indeed we did," she agreed provocatively. "In fact, we spent a delightful afternoon. You should have come with us after all, my lord."

"But then I fear the afternoon would have been somewhat less delightful if I had, for my curricle was not designed to carry three," pointed out his lordship.

Walter gave a bark of laughter at that, which caused his stepdaughter to flush up and shoot him a glance of acute dislike. But Mr. FitzSimmons said instantly, "I, at least, would have found it a great deal less delightful, I must confess. In fact, not to mince matters, you would have been decidedly in the way, old friend."

"But then I shall have my revenge tomorrow," insisted his lordship in amusement. "For I shall take Miss Morden out, and *you* shall stay at home."

Livia laughed delightedly, well pleased. She was in her best looks, wearing one of her newest and most expensive gowns, and had been determinedly flirting with his lordship all evening.

Sorrel guessed unkindly that it was all designed to fully subjugate him again. It was unlikely she had been pleased at his unaccountable defection that afternoon; but the visit was rapidly coming to a close, and she was clearly on her best behavior. Perhaps it had at last begun to dawn on her that for once she had mistaken her man, and all her tricks and starts were not working as she was used to.

There did indeed seem to be a speculative light in her eyes as they rested on him, but she said carelessly now, "What on earth did you find to do all afternoon, my lord?"

"Oh, I promise you I spent a most agreeable day myself," said his lordship smoothly. "Miss Kent took pity upon me and very kindly showed me the church."

Sorrel had been only half attending to their nonsense, but that jerked her head upright, and she felt the betraying color invade her cheeks. She cast his lordship an accusing glance, very aware of her cousin's sudden frown, and said calmly, "His lordship is merely being polite, I'm afraid. He can't have found it—very interesting."

But his lordship seemed to be in a mood of devilry for some reason, for he said promptly, "As usual, you are too modest, ma'am! On the contrary, I found the afternoon—most enlightening, in more ways than one. You must know, Miss Morden, that your cousin has a very well-informed mind, and I find her ideas as unusual as they are refreshing."

Sorrel tried to frown him down again. She could not imagine what he thought he was doing—other than maliciously taking his revenge for Livia's attempts to make him jealous—but he should have known her cousin would scarcely take even such tepid praise of another woman in good part. Indeed, she uttered a dangerous titter, her good intentions evidently already forgotten, and said with false admiration, "Oh, I am sure she is quite a paragon! Mama is forever praising her to the skies, but I confess that to be forever boring on about churches and antiquities and such is of little interest to me."

"Now, lovey," said Aunt Lela unhappily, "it would do you no harm to read a book now and then, for all that I am not bookish myself. Besides, his lordship is right, Sorrel indeed has a most refreshing mind, for I've often noted it myself. And I am sure I have enjoyed her visit even more than I expected to, and shall be sorry when she leaves us."

But at that Sorrel had to laugh reluctantly. "Thank you, ma'am, but I very much fear that my cousin is right, and I am a hopeless case. Indeed, my mama was obliged to give up on me years ago." She hesitated, then added defiantly, and for his lordship's ears alone, "But I am glad you have brought up the subject of my returning home, ma'am, for indeed I must be thinking of that soon, you know."

Aunt Lela instantly protested against that. "I hope you know that's not what I meant, my love! Indeed, I had hoped you might stay for a year at least."

From her cousin's face she did not share that hope. But Sorrel said merely, "Thank you, ma'am. But I have a life at home, remember. In fact, perhaps now would be as good a time as any to confess that my cousin is right in her estimation of me. I have come to the same conclusion, and when I return home, I am thinking seriously of opening a school." This time she met his lordship's eyes fully, her pride wanting him to see that she was unaffected by the afternoon, and had a life of her own.

But it was her aunt who reacted most strongly to this pronouncement. "Open a school?" she repeated in the same shocked tone she might have used if Sorrel had announced she was planning on opening a brothel instead. "No, no! Oh, my love, if I thought you were in the least serious I would—" she broke off, looking in trouble between her daughter and the marquis, for some reason. Then she seemed to pull herself together and went on more temperately, "Oh, but you must be teasing us! Besides, I am sure your papa would never permit you to do such a thing."

"But then it is not in his power to prevent me, ma'am. I shall be one-and-twenty soon, and I have an income left me by my paternal grandmother."

Her aunt looked even more troubled, but remained silent. It was Livia who said with false enthusiasm, "Why, I think that would be the very thing for you, cousin!"

When her mama remonstrated with her rather sharply, she looked around innocently. "Why, what have I said? She says herself she is unlikely to marry now, after the death of her fiancé. And since she seems to care nothing for balls and parties and such, I think it is the perfect solution."

"Nonsense!" said Aunt Lela impatiently. "It is ridiculous to talk of her as if she were already on the shelf. Of course she will marry."

She then firmly changed the subject, beginning to talk of the ball they were to attend the next day in Cheltenham and the arrangements that had been made. Aunt Lela had been at last persuaded, and they were to drive over the next afternoon, putting up at a local hotel and attending the subscription ball at the new Rooms built for the purpose that evening. After inspecting the shops the next morning, they would drive back in the afternoon. If Sorrel thought her aunt had been right in her concerns that to drive a distance of some forty miles and back just to attend a ball was excessive, she was too wise to say so.

Livia certainly saw nothing to cavil at in so energetic a program. It was Aunt Lela who said, with another worried glance at her niece, "But what of you, my love? Do you think the drive will be too tiring for you?"

Sorrel was taken off guard. "But I do not mean to accompany you, ma'am!" she blurted out. "I mean—unless you wish me to, of course. But I certainly shall not be attending the ball."

Livia was looking displeased again, and said shortly, "Good God, Mama, where have your wits gone begging? Of course Sorrel will not dance all in her blacks. Have you forgotten she is still in mourning?"

But for once Aunt Lela refused to bow to her daughter's dictates. "No, I have not forgotten. But I have been thinking about that, and while I do not mean to offend you, my dear, I understand it is very nearly a year now since that poor young man died, and it is time you were going out into the world a little again. Especially if you are talking of something so nonsensical as opening a school. No, no, just hear me out, my dear. There will be not a soul present who knows you, or who will be in the least shocked, and indeed I would not have agreed to the scheme at all if I had thought that you would not accompany us, my love. Besides, you will make the numbers up, for I am sure Livia, much as she might long to, can scarcely dance with two gentlemen at the same time."

Chapter 16

Sorrel was a little taken aback, as much by her aunt's sly dig at her beautiful daughter, which was unusual, as by her suggestion. She had been glad enough for the excuse of her mourning to escape going to London balls and parties, but it was true that she saw little value in the strict mourning period of one year dictated by society. The wearing of black or the absence of it did not in any way affect her own grief, and she knew she had long since ceased to grieve poor William. He seemed, in fact, part of another life, and one a long time in the past that had little to do with her now.

But she said quickly now, "No, no, I am content to remain at home. Besides, there will be other young ladies at the ball. And now that I come to think of it, I feel very sure that I couldn't dance even if I were dying to, for the dances will scarcely be the same as I am used to at home."

Aunt Lela looked rather crestfallen at that, but the marquis said immediately, "That at least need not concern you, my dear Miss Kent. I would not attempt to argue against your scruples, but we can easily teach you to dance this evening, for I flatter myself you could not find better tutors. You must know Fitz is everywhere considered a master at the quadrille, and few perform it more gracefully, while I would be delighted to teach you to waltz. In fact, I propose we repair immediately to the music room, for there is clearly not a moment to be lost."

Livia was looking daggers at Sorrel again, but it was Walter who, with some malice, immediately took the suggestion up with enthusiasm. He pronounced himself perfectly willing to second his lordship in his tutoring efforts, and kindly volunteered his stepdaughter to accompany them on the pianoforte.

This was even less to Livia's liking, but fortunately she was rescued by her flustered mother. "No, no, for she will be needed to show Sorrel the steps. I shall play for them, though I fear I am more than rusty."

From that point Sorrel seemed powerless to halt the tide of events. She glared at the marquis, who smiled back at her blandly and seemed to deliberately misunderstand her reluctance. "Don't worry, Miss Kent! You will find that you soon catch on to the steps."

It seemed too late—not to mention hypocritical of her—to belatedly plead her conscience. In fact she could find no excuse at all, except the real one, which she naturally had no intention of confessing. But she had no wish to be held in the marquis's arms again, even in the movements of a dance.

She contented herself with remarking darkly that they might change their minds after they had seen her dance. But indeed the quadrille, which Mr. FitzSimmons so gracefully demonstrated for her with Livia's reluctant help, was not dissimilar to a dance they did at home and Sorrel caught on quickly. She had never shone in a ballroom, especially if her mother was there, but she was graceful and a quick learner, and it was not long before she had mastered the basic steps—though she felt wooden enough with all eyes upon her and could have cursed the marquis for the suggestion.

But Aunt Lela played happily, if somewhat erratically, and even Walter stayed to mark the time, while they went through an entire dance to practice. The marquis soon led Livia out to join them, so that the session turned almost into an impromptu ball, which made Livia's humor improve slightly. After all, she had his lordship for her own partner, and was able point out the many mistakes that Sorrel made, which did much to put her back into a good temper.

But when it came time for the marquis to teach Sorrel the steps of the waltz, she was clearly less pleased. She happily whirled around the room once or twice in his arms to demonstrate the dance for Sorrel, but did not appreciate the fact that both the marquis and Mr. FitzSimmons then threw themselves enthusiastically into teaching her dull American cousin the steps. Even Walter called out instructions and corrections from time to time, and hummed along with the music, slightly off-key.

The waltz had not yet made its way to America, and at first, with his lordship's arm about her waist, and his face so close to her own, Sorrel was even more wooden, and frequently had to apologize for treading on his toes. But he merely laughed and made her dance on, and gradually she relaxed as she caught on to the steps. She had to admit that he was indeed an excellent dancer, and she soon unwillingly allowed herself to be caught up in the exhilaration of gliding and turning so smoothly in his arms. While Aunt Lela played a lilting waltz tune, and Mr. FitzSimmons and Walter looked on critically, she was able to waltz gracefully about the room without disgracing herself too much.

It naturally did not occur to her that she looked at her best, with her cheeks glowing with exercise and her steps quickly adjusting themselves gracefully to his lordship's lead, until Walter declared even more maliciously, with a sly glance at his stepdaughter, "By Jove, Miss Kent, you have been hiding your light under a bushel! You will take the shine out of everyone tomorrow night, including this stepdaughter of mine! Demme if I ever saw the waltz danced more gracefully."

That made her falter again, for Livia was looking daggers at her, and without another word abruptly turned and walked out of the room. But it was perhaps as well she did, for the marquis was smiling down at her in a way that Livia could scarcely have missed, and said softly, for Sorrel's ears alone. "For once your esteemed stepuncle is right! Either I am a better instructor than I believed myself, or you are an excellent pupil. I claim the right of dancing the first waltz with you tomorrow night, my dear Sorrel. Besides, you did not really think I would leave you behind to get into any more danger, did you?"

Sorrel, breathless, could think of not a word to say in reply.

Despite everything, she liked Cheltenham, with its Regency terraces and myriad of shop windows displaying every conceivable luxury. At the last minute Walter had declined to accompany them, saying that dancing was not in his line, and besides, he rather thought he would drive over and drop in on some friends in the district.

Aunt Lela had regarded this suggestion with suspicion, having reason to dislike any friends of his on principle. But before her guests she could say nothing, and so merely closed her lips tightly.

The drive was uneventful, and if Sorrel had feared Livia's temper, after the evening before, for once she was pleasantly surprised. Livia had come down in a thoughtful mood, and attired in her most becoming traveling dress. Now and then Sorrel caught her narrowed eyes upon her, as if her thoughts were none too pleasant. But at least she kept these to herself and did not break out into open warfare.

She graciously pronounced herself pleased with Cheltenham, especially the shops, and purchased any number of elegant trifles that she had no use for, or it would shortly be discovered did not at all become her. Her drawers were already crammed full of such things as the cunning little flower holders she found in one shop, which Sorrel did not doubt she would afterward decide were quite hideous, or the Indian silk shawl, which was really dog-cheap and thus not to be resisted, although it was a shame it was so ugly. But Sorrel was too grateful for her relatively benign mood to object to being dragged from shop to shop in her cousin's wake.

Aunt Lela, too, had not the least objection to paying for these objects, and indeed purchased several caps and a turban for herself. She tried to convince Sorrel to buy a pair of jet beads that would go well with her gray silk, and a chip-straw hat with a quantity of cherries on it that she assured her became her charmingly.

But when Sorrel resolutely passed over these tempting objects, Aunt Livia was brought to own that the jet beads were really very trumpery after all, for beads were not at all the thing; and the chip-straw had perhaps been a little vulgar, although one might have replaced the cherries with something more becoming, and thus had a very pretty hat.

Sorrel collected, from these various episodes, that with both her aunt and cousin the acquiring, and not the possessing, were the chief attractions, and so bore very well with Livia purchasing a dozen pairs of lace mitts, when she had a drawerful already, and really a very pretty pearl and sapphire pin, which would have been exactly what she had been looking for if only it had not been so small and the sapphires quite inferior.

And so the day passed surprisingly well, the men having taken themselves off on their own devices, and even Aunt Lela able to forget for whole stretches of half an hour or more her errant husband and what he might be getting up to. In fact, she strongly suspected he had taken the opportunity of attending the prizefight he had mentioned earlier, and if so, it was more than likely that he would return a good deal lighter in the pocket than when he had left, and probably stale-drunk.

They gathered again at the hotel for dinner, served in an elegant private parlor, and the only occurrence that risked marring the harmony of the day, and the expectations of a pleasant evening to come, was when Livia caught sight for the first time of Sorrel's gown.

It was the first time she had been out of her blacks in almost a year, and it felt strange to her. But it did not occur to her that Livia would be jealous of her gown; especially since Livia's own was by one of the foremost mantuamakers in London, and Sorrel happened to know exactly how much it had cost. It was of a celestial blue, with an overdress of white lace, and as usual made her cousin look enchantingly beautiful.

But Livia took one look at Sorrel's gown of simple cherry silk and began to frown heavily. "Where did you get that dress?" she demanded abruptly. "No simple Colonial dressmaker made that!"

Sorrel had already begun to regret giving in to her aunt's insistence, and wished she were back in her retiring black silks. Balls were by no means favorite with her, and she should have insisted on staying in her bedchamber with a good book. But she said indifferently, "No, it came from Paris. Papa bought it for me last year when he was over there. How well that blue becomes you, cousin! Dearest Aunt, doesn't Livia look enchanting?"

But for once Livia was not to be distracted. "Paris!" she exclaimed, obviously furious. The protracted war with France had made Paris gowns wholly unobtainable in England for years. "Well, at least Wycherly will be less than pleased, when he finds out it's French-made!" she announced in vindictive triumph, and swept on down the stairs.

She took the first opportunity of passing on this information to him, saying in a lull in the dinner conversation, after Mr. FitzSimmons had complimented both on their charming gowns, "Oh, I am quite cast into the shade by my dark-horse cousin! But then it is little wonder, since her gown came straight from Paris. I knew you, my lord, would find that less than amusing, since you have spent so many years of your life fighting the French."

Sorrel flushed, but the marquis said calmly, "My quarrel is with the French habit of taking over countries, not their fashions—especially when they are as charming as this. Mrs. Granville, will you take some wine?"

Livia flushed and cast an even more resentful glance at her cousin. But after that his lordship seemed to devote himself to amusing her, and under his expert charm she melted almost visibly, though still casting a frowning glance at Sorrel from time to time.

For her part Sorrel sat back and left it to him, wishing more than ever that she had had the sense to remain at home. At least once they entered the elegant subscription rooms where the ball was being held, Livia quickly became the center of attention, which improved her mood still more. But for herself, Sorrel felt exactly as if she were stepping back in time and were a tongue-tied sixteen-year-old girl again, however much she tried to remind herself she was older and more self-assured now, and in England, not America. The rooms were too hot, and too crowded, and it did not help that she knew not a soul there and had her cousin furious with her besides.

Livia, with a smug glance at her cousin, danced the first set of country dances with the marquis; and the second, a quadrille, with Mr. FitzSimmons. But after that she was inundated with partners, as usual.

Sorrel had no intention of trying to compete with her cousin, and had refused Mr. FitzSimmons for the country dances. She remained firmly beside her aunt, who was beaming with simple pride at her daughter's success, and remarked several times on what a handsome couple her daughter and the marquis made. She was plainly reveling in her triumph as well, especially in having so handsome and noble a guest in her party. It seemed likely that she was remembering earlier days, when her gowns had been homemade, not from the most expensive London modiste, and she had received more than a few snubs.

Even Sorrel's hand was solicited several more times by strange gentlemen, but the marquis was not among them. These all she resolutely declined, insisting to her disappointed aunt that she might have put off her mourning for the evening and consented to come to the ball, but she had no intention of dancing.

Aunt Lela took this well enough, and since she was a kindly creature and must have guessed some of what Sorrel was feeling, happily did not press her.

Sorrel told herself that she was glad the marquis did not approach her, despite his half-veiled threat of the night before. Livia was suspicious already, and perhaps he realized he had tried her too far. In any event, after dancing with Livia he very properly and with unexpected kindness stood up with a shy child who was sitting unnoticed, and then even more properly led out the wife of one of the dignitaries of the town whom they had been introduced to on arrival.

It was not until the chords of the first waltz sounded that he came toward Sorrel, with his irresistible smile. "Miss Kent, will you do me the honor? I believe I bespoke the first waltz and here I am to claim it."

Sorrel glanced quickly at her aunt, whose attention was momentarily distracted, and even more quickly around for her cousin, whom she suspected had had every intention of dancing the first waltz with the marquis. She said hastily and with something less than tact, "No, no! I m'-mean, thank you, my lord, but I am not dancing tonight. You should ask my cousin!"

He, too, glanced where Livia stood surrounded by her usual throng, and said patiently, "I have already done my duty by your cousin. Nor will I be missed in that crowd, I promise you. And I am well aware you are not dancing tonight—though I am wholly in the dark as to the reason. You may explain it to me while we are dancing. Come, Miss Kent! You should know by now I am not so easy to fob off as the others seem to be, and I mean to redeem your promise."

Aunt Lela had glanced back, and was nodding and smiling. Sorrel got reluctantly to her feet, but said in a heated undertone, "I made you no such promise, as you very well know, my lord! And I do not care to make a fool of myself in such a crowd. Go and dance with my cousin and leave me alone!"

He ignored her and took her wrist in a peremptory grasp, which reminded her too sharply of that fatal afternoon, and placed it on his arm. Short of struggling openly she had no choice but to go with him, and her cheeks hot with temper, allowed him to lead her onto the floor.

As she went, she caught her cousin's expression as it rested upon them. It was not a pleasant one, and did not bode well for the next day.

As soon as the music had begun and he had swept her into the dance, Sorrel said irritably, "You may find it amusing to cause trouble between my cousin and me, my lord, but I do not."

She knew already he was an excellent dancer, and it would seem he was an even more excellent instructor, for somewhat to her surprise, even while distracted and angry, she had no trouble fitting her steps to his.

He glanced down at her with the smile in his eyes she found so hard to resist, and said a little ruefully, "Unjust, Miss Kent! Especially when I have been at such pains tonight to *not* cause trouble between you and your cousin. Why else do you think I stayed away from you so long? I even refrained from telling you how enchanting you look tonight in your Paris gown. You should always wear such vivid colors, for it makes you look a different creature entirely. I scarcely recognized you when you first came down."

Her cheeks had warmed a little under his unexpected praise, but she said quite crossly, "Thank you! You did not need to remind me that I usually fade into the woodwork, for you have told me so already! And I begin to think you are an accomplished flirt, my lord."

"I know you do," he acknowledged even more ruefully. "I have tried to discover what I could have done to earn that unkind and unfair estimation, and can only think it is your unnatural prejudice against my rank. When have I ever flirted with you, for instance?"

She almost gasped. "Well, if it is not flirting to—" Then she broke off, too late, annoyed with her wretched tongue and blushing fierily.

He laughed. "Ah, unwise, Miss Kent! But if you are referring to my kissing you, as by your blushes I have no doubt you are, you are mistaken. I had no intention of flirting with you then, or at any other time."

"Good God, don't talk so loudly!" she begged, looking around herself in embarrassment. "Pray let us talk of something else. Or nothing at all, for I still need to mind my steps."

"You lie, Miss Kent! At the risk of sounding vain, it would seem I am an excellent teacher, for you dance better than anyone else in the room, and have not the least need to mind your steps. And I've not the least objection to anyone hearing me."

But that was too ingenuous to be believed, and she could not prevent herself from looking pointedly where her cousin was waltzing with Mr. FitzSimmons, looking the picture of grace and beauty. "I will forbear to put that to the test, my lord, as you must have counted on!" she said scornfully. "But you may leave me right out of whatever game you are playing with my cousin, for I do not find it in the least amusing."

"It is you who are playing games, Miss Kent. Everything I have done is entirely consistent, if you can but bring yourself to believe it." He did not wait for her to answer—which was just as well—but also looked over to where Livia was, and added dryly, "Your cousin is certainly beautiful, and no one would dispute the fact that she is the center of attention. But it seems to me you have received a number of invitations to dance yourself tonight. Why did you not accept them? And don't tell me that you are still in mourning, for despite what you think me, I am not a fool."

She was beginning to think him anything but, but said with mockery, "Yes, it is amazing the flattering attention I receive when in my cousin's company—all from men hoping I will introduce them to my beautiful and wealthy cousin and who would be hard-pressed to recognize me the next day if they encountered me on my own. It is quite a wonder that my head is not turned completely."

Then she was sorry to have said so much, for there was unexpected understanding in his eyes, and his hand tightened momentarily on hers. "Yes, I know Miss Sorrel Kent finds nothing in herself that might attract a man," he said. "But I will give you two to be going on with. You have brains and you have courage, more than I have ever known in a woman before. Is it so unlikely that a man might find those preferable to a mere pretty face?"

Instead of responding with frozen dignity, as she should have, she said bitterly, "But I think even you will admit, my lord, that brains and courage are of very little use in a ballroom."

He laughed. "Perhaps. But one spends so little of one's life in the ballroom. Have you thought of that? And I will give you something else to think of, Miss Sorrel Kent. For all her beauty I have never even been tempted to kiss your cousin. Does that satisfy you?"

Chapter 17

Sorrel flushed, and looked away. "And do you expect me to believe that?" she demanded even more bitterly. Then she added, too late, "Or that I care in the least whom you may kiss?"

The laughter abruptly faded from his face, and he looked almost stern. "Odd as it may seem, I do expect you to believe it."

But that was expecting too much of her. There had been a certain exhilaration in sparring with him, even angry as she had been, but suddenly she felt merely weary and longed for the evening to be over. "I don't know what your game may be, my lord," she said quietly. "Or why, for some reason it amuses you to tease me. But I neither wish for your pity nor mean to become a pawn in whatever game you may be playing with my cousin. And now take me back to my aunt, if you please. I have the headache, a little, and have no more wish to dance."

After a moment he shrugged, and did as she bid. But he had the last word, after all. "I will obey—for the present, Miss Kent. But I neither feel in the least sorry for you, nor have any need to make your cousin jealous. I might add that I have every intention of making you own that in the end. But since while I am still a guest in your aunt's house my position is somewhat awkward, I will say no more—for the present. But there still remains a day of reckoning to come between us. And I have not forgotten that I promised myself I would make you trust

me someday——of your own free will and without any co-
ercion on my part. Now I must thank you for a delightful
dance, and hope your headache will soon be better."

He bowed and returned her to her aunt and did not remain long by their side. Sorrel had the doubtful felicity
of seeing him make his way straight to her cousin's side,
and he seldom left it thereafter.

She told herself firmly that she was pleased, for the
marquis's attentions, whatever his motive, could only
cause further trouble for her. Let him marry Livia and be
done with it, and leave her alone.

But despite her brave words, she was not in the least
surprised to discover, a little later, that the headache she
had claimed had become a reality. But then it was
scarcely surprising, for she had always hated balls, with
their loud music and hot rooms and the need to keep a
smile pinned on one's face when one was longing only
for one's room and a little oblivion. She had been a fool
to allow herself to be dragged to this one, against her
better judgment and all past experience. She would
never attend one again.

But she should have known the evening was not quite
done with her yet.

As she wearily discarded her fine Paris gown some
hours later, there was a brief scratch at the door, and her
cousin entered, already in her expensive silk wrapper,
and yawning with tiredness.

They were not on such terms that included bedtime
chats, and so Sorrel greeted her warily. But Livia seemed
to be in an unexpected mood, roaming around the hotel
bedchamber, and talking idly of the ball.

Sorrel endured it, though her head was aching in
earnest by then and she longed only for her bed. But at
last Livia seemed to have come to the end, for she added
with more meaning, "But did you enjoy it, cousin? As
Mama keeps reminding me, it is, after all, to show you a

good time during your visit to England that we came to this benighted part of the country."

"Yes, I enjoyed it very well, thank you."

Livia laughed at the polite words and carelessly sat down on the end of the bed. "Some parts of it more than others, I would guess, cousin! But do you seriously imagine that Wycherly is interested in you?"

So that was it. But then it was no more than Sorrel had expected. "No," she said wearily. "I don't."

At least she had the satisfaction of seeing Livia look a little startled. "Oh, well, that's all right then. For you know he is going to marry me, of course."

Sorrel's heart jumped, but she would not give her cousin any further reason to suspect her. "I must congratulate you, then. When is the wedding to be?" she inquired even more politely.

Livia looked slightly discomfited, but she recovered quickly and shrugged one beautiful shoulder. "Soon, you may be sure. I have every intention of marrying him, and I always get what I want."

"How lucky for you. But what has any of this to do with me?"

"Nothing, of course. We have not spent a great deal of time together, but we are cousins, after all." Abruptly she yawned and jumped to her feet again. "But it is late, and I'm sure you're tired."

As she trailed toward the door in her wrapper, she added artlessly, "I daresay you meant it and you will be going home soon? Back to America, I mean? As you said, you cannot remain forever, and I'm sure you must be longing to get back to your own life. This time in England has merely been a diversion for you. I make no doubt you think we are all vain and shallow and fools."

For the first time Sorrel actually felt like laughing. So that was what all this had been about. "Yes, fairly soon," she agreed, and did not bother to contradict the last part of Livia's statement.

Livia gave her a brilliant smile. "That's all right then. Good night, cousin."

For once Sorrel was no longer willing to let her have it all her own way. "One moment—cousin," she said abruptly. "You sought out this interview, not I, so you may answer a question for me. Why is it so important to you to marry a title?" She asked it with real curiosity.

Livia didn't answer her directly. Instead she busied herself with winding one of the ribbons from her wrapper around her finger, and said obliquely, "You don't like me, do you, cousin? It offends you that I go around saying what others only think. But have you ever considered, with your disapproving airs and your silent assurance, that things were easier for you than they were for me, despite my beauty? Your papa, after all, was someone who was respected and admired. Mine was kind and cheerful, but even I could tell he was crude in his manners and despised even by our expensive butler at the time. My next stepfather was even more wealthy, and doted on me. I could wrap him round my little finger without the least effort, and he would buy me anything I merely expressed the slightest desire to possess." Even now she could not resist boasting a little. Then she made a moue of distaste. "But he was no more respectable than my own father had been, and on the whole I was relieved he died before I was old enough to make my come-out. There's no doubt he would have embarrassed me and jeopardized my chances."

She added indifferently, "You don't like that, I can see, but then you never had to cringe with embarrassment, or be looked down on by the other girls at school, even though my papa could have bought and sold theirs easily. Was that fair? None of them were as beautiful as I was, but they looked down at me for who my parents were, and scarcely troubled to hide it. Well, you may be sure that is something I mean never to endure again. When I am Lady Wycherly we shall see how they laugh and hold up their noses to me then!"

Sorrel listened to this jumbled mixture of pathos and vindictiveness, bathos and boasting, and scarcely knew whether to be repelled or pity her beautiful cousin. But at least she perhaps came closer to understanding her than she had done before. She could not sympathize with many of her motives, but nor could she any longer despise her as she had been doing, and it was easy enough to see what had made her the way she was. It seemed Sorrel herself, with her own tumbled feelings of love and jealousy toward her own mother, and her woeful feelings of inadequacy, had still had it easier than she had thought.

And maybe her cousin was right, and the answer was as simple as buying yourself a title and lording it over those who had snubbed you in the past.

When she said nothing, Livia added with unexpected shrewdness, "Perhaps it is just as well we had this little talk, for I think we understand each other better than we did. Mama hoped we would become friends, but we are much too different for that. But for all I may seem to lack your prickly independence, I have every intention of running my life exactly as I choose. People tend to dismiss me, because I am beautiful, you know. But I am quite as practical as my mother, and I know exactly what I want. And I can be dangerous when crossed, so remember that, cousin. And now it is late, and I am going to bed. But remember what I said, for I warn you I won't let anything—*anything*—stand in my way."

She was gone on the words, and Sorrel was left blinking after her, and to make what she could of the few night hours left to her.

The return drive the next morning was without incident. Aunt Lela frankly dozed most of the way, and Sorrel was glad enough to close her eyes and pretend sleep, to avoid any further tête-à-tête with her beautiful cousin. She felt that, as Livia had said, all that needed to be ex-

pressed between them had been done, and there was little left to say.

The next few days passed uneventfully as well. Walter, returned from his visit in a foul mood that indeed
suggested his luck had been quite out, and began to
throw scarcely veiled hints that the marquis's visit was
drawing to a close and he had yet to drop his handkerchief.

"Which don't surprise me in the least!" he said unpleasantly. "With no more entertainment offered than a
country dance and a few expeditions to see local sights
that he's not the least interested in seeing, and the lure of
fair Livia's beauty, it's no wonder he's having second
thoughts. A fortnight of her unadulterated company
would be enough for anyone! Well, all I can say is that
you have managed it damned badly, between the two of
you, and it's not likely you'll get such an opportunity
again! But then I might have known that your shabby-
genteel notions would betray you in the end, for haven't
I been victim enough of them myself? Did you really
think to bring Wycherly up to scratch with your nip-
cheese dinner parties and country routs? You'd have
done much better to attend to me, instead of thinking
you always know best, and looking down you nose at me
in that disapproving way."

Sorrel entered inadvertently into this marital squabble
in time to hear her aunt saying shrilly, "I'll have you
know that there's nothing nip-cheese about me! And as
for you, coming back with your tail between your legs, I
make no doubt, for all your grand pronouncements, and
then telling me how I should behave toward my guests
as if you were infinitely superior to me, it's enough to
make me laugh! Yes, you'd like me to believe you and
his lordship are bosom bows, no doubt, but if you ask
me, he knows exactly what you are, and is laughing at
you behind your back, for all his good manners. Certainly the whole world knows that it's my money that
enables you to make your fashionable appearance about

town, and my money you squander on every prizefight or race or game of chance that comes along! And if you do or say anything to ruin my Livy's chances, then you may find you've cozened me for the last time!"

Walter, taking refuge in a superiority that even Sorrel found odious, said scathingly, "Ruin her chances! That's rich. From aught I can tell, she's done that herself, with her tricks and starts, thinking to reel him in easily like all the other fools who are in love with her. Well, he's more sense than that, which I could have told her, and if we are to talk of seeing through people, it's my bet that he knows her for exactly the spoiled little termagant she is! I should know, for I've had to put up with it for years, and if you think that's been easy, you're mistaken! As for ruining her chances, the sooner you marry her off, the better I'll be pleased. Though if I had a spark of decency I'd warn the poor fellow what a cunning little spitfire she is before it's too late. Not that I suspect he needs any warning."

Before Aunt Lela could open her mouth to escalate the warfare, Sorrel intervened hurriedly, "For God's sake, hush! You can be heard throughout the house, and I doubt either of you think that is likely to amuse his lordship."

Aunt Lela dutifully lowered her voice, but said resentfully, "And now you see how your fine sensibilities have helped us! But when it comes to insulting my daughter, it is the outside of enough, and more than flesh and blood can stand.

"Oh, I know well no one's wishes count but her own! You keep me on a damned short leash, and grudge me every penny, but whatever Her Highness wishes is instantly procured."

"Aye, and if you had more pride than to batten on your wife, I'd think the better of you for it! *Nor* will you cozen me into believing that you only came back to help me. That's rich! I declare, I made the greatest mistake of my life when I married you, and I have to live with it, for a scandal I won't have to ruin my daughter's future. But not one penny more will you get from me, until next quarter, and so I warn you."

"There's gratitude for you," said Mr. Granville bitterly. "Here I abandon a most convivial gathering of my own to post to your rescue, and it's as well I did, for between the pair of you, you and your precious daughter, you're making a regular bumblebroth of it! And when you've succeeded in queering your pitch with one of the wealthiest peers in the land, don't look to me for pity!"

Aunt Lela reared up as if he had struck her. "Pity? I would never look to you for so human an emotion! We did very well before you came, and if you do anything to queer my Livy's chances—I'll—I'll—well, I don't know what I'll do, but it will be bad, I can promise you. And then I'll divorce you, scandal or no scandal!"

They always quarreled, but it was unlike her aunt to get so worked up. Sorrel glanced at her quickly, longing to escape, but not liking to leave her aunt alone.

"Aye, pretty talking," said Walter bitterly. "Though God knows I've come to expect no better from you. But it's the Luscious Livia you have to fear, not me. Haven't I told you it will suit me very well to be nearly related to Wycherly? And that I've a scheme in foot that will make my fortune, and free me from being dependent upon you for every groat I spend? As for needing money from you, that just goes to show how you constantly misjudge me, for I'm very well beforehand with the world. Won a monkey from old Makepiece only shortly before I came."

"And lost it again the day after, I make no doubt. As for this precious scheme of yours, ten to one it has something to do either with horses or a run of luck with the dice, which I take leave to inform you is scarcely a sound investment and is bound to end in ruin."

Walter once more began to look odiously superior. "Well, that just shows all you know. All I can tell you is that I'm in a fair way to pulling it off, and if I do I shall be independent of you forever. Which, I must tell you, would be a very good thing, and could scarcely please you more than it does me!"

Aunt Lela surprised them both very much by bursting into tears. "Well, if I've misjudged you for once, I'm sure I'm sorry! But when it comes to you maligning my daughter, and implying it's my fault his lordship hasn't popped the question yet, it's almost more than I can bear! As for accusing me of grudging you every penny, and behaving hard-fisted toward you, if I do, it's a little wonder, for well I know you only married me for my money."

Walter looked horrified, and quickly beat a hasty retreat, leaving Sorrel to regard her aunt with sudden concern. It was indeed unlike her to react so strongly, especially where her husband was concerned. Sorrel could only think Walter had hit a little too close to the bone, for she had feared for days that Aunt Lela was worried about the marquis's failure to make Livia an offer.

Now she said inadequately, "Aunt! Don't. He's not worth it. Why, I've never known you to cry over him before."

Aunt Lela mopped her eyes and blew her nose determinedly. "Nor I wouldn't now! What, cry over that twiddle-faced, tallowpoop? It's not likely! It's just one thing and another. Dearest, you weren't serious the other day about starting a school, were you?"

"Why, surely you're not crying over that?"

"No, I told you it just seems like everything's too much, of a sudden. Walter's right, I may have bungled things, for here's his lordship not made Livy an offer, despite everything, and his visit's almost up now. And needless to say she's fair spitting nails because of it, and blaming me, and what with Walter sticking his nasty nose into everything and acting superior, and now you behaving as if you were one-and-forty instead of not quite one-and-twenty, and already firmly on the shelf, I'm sure it's not surprising if I'm not myself."

"But, Aunt," said Sorrel, still mystified, "if his lordship has not yet made Livia an offer, that's scarcely your fault, whatever they may say. And as for me——" Then she stopped, and said in sudden enlightenment, "Oh, dear! Have you received another blackmail threat?"

Aunt Lela blew her nose again and turned toward her a little blindly. "Yes, and just when I had begun to believe—oh, I almost begin to regret ever inviting his lordship, for Walter's right, nothing has turned out as I planned it. And now this will have to be paid, though I'm sure I hope you know that whatever Walter may say, I'm not one of them nasty, nip-farthings, grudging every groat and making and scraping. It's just that everything seems too much, of a sudden."

"I—have been expecting this," said Sorrel. "Did he name a time and place for the money to be delivered this time?"

Chapter 18

"Yes," said her aunt. "And what's more, my love, he claims that there have been two attempts on your life already. Dearest, why didn't you tell me? I may be a bad mother, and an even worse aunt, but did you seriously think I would let anything—including my daughter's happiness—stand in the way of protecting you?"

Sorrel felt ashamed. "No, no! Of course I didn't. How could you think it after you have been so kind to me? What I did think was that you would do exactly what you are doing, which will answer nothing."

"I know that, but I can't and won't risk your life for so paltry a sum, my love!"

Sorrel said slowly, knowing she needed to tread warily, "Perhaps. How is the money to be paid, ma'am?"

"What's that got to do with it? I am to take it to a nearby wood and leave it there. He even sent a map of sorts. Well, I never thought to be grateful that Walter was here, but he may at least prove useful for once. He may take the money, and then there will be an end to it! I begin to think nothing is as I believed it, and I am almost sorry we came back here. Everything seems to have gone wrong since we did."

But Sorrel scarcely heard her aunt, for she had just experienced something in the nature of a revelation. She had already decided it had to be someone who knew her aunt well, and when it came to it, who knew her better than Walter? Walter, who was always in debt; Walter who had begun to resent more and more his wife's hold on the purse strings. Walter, who had declared loftily more than once in her hearing that he had finally hit upon a scheme to solve all his money worries.

Still, Sorrel checked her rising certainty, not quite prepared yet to believe that even Walter could stoop so low, and mend his fortunes on her aunt's distress and worry.

But the more she considered it, the less she was able to dismiss it, monstrous though it might be. Walter was exactly the sort to find it amusing to blackmail his own wife to obtain the funds which otherwise he would have to wheedle and beg from her——and was increasingly uncertain of obtaining, for even to Sorrel it was clear that her aunt's patience had almost run out.

She was both slightly relieved and even more outraged at so simple a solution. It had been bad enough when she had thought it a stranger, or one of the servants. But Walter to blackmail his own wife and make her so unhappy. Walter to threaten her own and Livia's safety——knowing exactly how much his wife and stepdaughter desired the marquis's visit to go perfectly, and how much they would pay to keep anything from happening to mar it and risk Livia's future.

Walter who had appeared unexpectedly only a few days before the final letter was delivered, setting out the method of payment.

And Walter, who it appeared had twice come close to injuring her or even killing her, without compunction or hesitation.

It was still unclear to Sorrel why he had singled her out for his attempts. But then, however much he disliked his stepdaughter, very likely he did not dare risk Livia's safety. With Livia dead or seriously injured, he would have lost all hold over his wealthy wife. Aunt Lela had said many times that without Livia's future to worry about, she wouldn't have hesitated to divorce Walter long ago.

Sorrel discovered that despite her earlier words of caution, she had already accepted it as the truth, for everything fitted so well. And if so, relief suddenly won out over outrage, for they were no longer dealing with someone who might be a dangerous enemy, but only Walter, whom she could not in the least take seriously. In fact, even anger was rapidly losing out to amusement, for it was indeed exactly like him.

After a moment she said even more carefully, uncertain of how much to confide in her aunt at this point, "I beg your pardon, ma'am, but do you think it—wise to trust Walter to take the money?"

Her aunt stared at her, and took her up in a way Sorrel had not anticipated. "Good God! Do you think he would say the money was delivered, and then make off with it himself? But then where have my wits gone begging? That's exactly what he would do! Oh, and to think I had no more sense than to be taken in by his fine airs and noble name! After two husbands you'd have thought I'd have more sense, and so I should have. Well, you're right, my love, and it's you who has the head on her shoulders. But what's to be done? At least I am still adamant that it must be paid, but to go traipsing around in some wood at my time of life I can't and won't do, and that's final. Well, I shall just have to find some other way, for whatever you say, my love, I can't help but blame myself. If I had done it at the beginning, you might have been spared considerable danger."

"I could take it myself," offered Sorrel, the beginnings of a plan in mind. "No, dearest Aunt, only hear me out! I don't think there will be so very much of a risk after all."

Aunt Lela naturally exclaimed against that, but as Sorrel had expected, it was not very different to persuade her in the end of so outrageous a theory. When she had finished, her aunt sat back and said with conviction and considerable bitterness, "Heaven help me, that is exactly what he would do! No wonder he turned up so pat! And when I think of the danger he put you in, and the heartache he has caused me, it is almost more than I can bear! The audacity! And then sitting in this very room boasting that he had found a way to solve his financial problems. Aye, he thought he had, and that he'd stumbled upon a neat little game I make no doubt! Not to mention a steady source of funds, for while I draw the line at financing his expensive gaming habits, he knew full well that where my daughter was concerned, I could be relied upon to lay down the blunt, and no questions asked. Oh, it makes my blood boil, only to think of it! Well, that settles it. I shall have to divorce him, and the scandal be damned."

"Wait, Aunt. I have another plan. If you divorce him now there will indeed be a scandal. Besides, he will only deny our suspicions, and we have no real proof. But were we to get that proof, you would have enough of a hold over him to be rid of him quietly, for what he has attempted is indeed illegal, and he could be arrested for it, and perhaps even transported."

"Aye, I daresay he could be, but he must know I would never take it that far," objected her aunt reluctantly. "I have come to despise him and will indeed be glad to be rid of him, but I wouldn't have him arrested, even though it's no more than he deserves. To think of taking advantage of my fears and aspirations, and playing such a cruel trick upon his own wife! It makes my blood boil whenever I think of it."

"I agree that the matter must be hushed up at all costs. Nor have I any more respect for him than you do. But I meant what I said about my taking the money to the rendezvous. Were we to catch him in the very act of collecting it, we might use it to your advantage for a little polite blackmail of our own. Whatever else we may think him, I believe him far too vain to ever stand his name being so blackened. And keep in mind that were you to divorce him in the usual way, not only would there be a considerable scandal, which will hardly do Livia any good, but he will undoubtedly demand a large sum of money from you, and probably get it."

"Yes, but it would be worth any amount to be rid of

him for good," said her aunt truthfully. "But you are right, my love. How glad I am that you came to visit me, for it's you who has the brains, indeed. I don't know what I'd have done without you. But although I agree with you that it would be a very good thing to catch him in the act, and I have not the least compunction about blackmailing him in turn, it is still out of the question! I will not let you take such a risk for my sake."

Sorrel, her eyes full of sudden mischief, set herself to coax her aunt to change her mind. She was herself not in the least afraid of Walter, and once she had realized who was behind the blackmail attempt, had lost all fear. In fact humor was well in the ascendance by now, though she was careful to hide it from her aunt. She found herself, in fact, at one point longing to share the cream of the jest with the marquis, for he was the one person she could count on to fully appreciate it.

But she did not mean to share it, of course. She had every confidence he would not be in the least scandalized, or even much shocked for all his noble title. But manlike, he would undoubtedly demand to take care of it himself, and Sorrel did not mean for anyone to spoil her adventure. Besides, her promise to her aunt still held. Less than ever would her aunt wish him to know that his future father-in-law was capable of such a contemptible and even criminal plot.

She succeeded so well in convincing her, that Aunt Lela at last said grudgingly, "Well, you are right that if it is only Walter you will scarcely be in any danger. Lord, when I think of how he gammoned me. *Me!* Who prides herself on her shrewdness and has married two fortunes in my day, to be taken in by such a jackstraw. And when I think from first to last what he's cost me already, and this is the thanks I get. Nor will I attempt to deny that it would give me a great deal of pleasure to outdo him at his own game and be rid of him for good and all. But to let you shoulder my burdens, and ride out alone don't seem right. You are my responsibility, my love, for your

mother entrusted you to me. I can't think what she'd say
if she knew I was even contemplating letting you do
such a thing."

"Dearest Aunt Lela," said Sorrel truthfully, "Mama
knows very well I am able to take care of myself. Besides, it will be in broad daylight, and whatever else I
may have thought about your mysterious blackmailer,
you may be sure I am not in the least afraid of Walter.
Besides, you can't be so unkind as to withdraw your permission now, for I warn you I mean to go, whatever you
say. I have been wondering how I can repay you for all
your kindness to me, and now I have found it."

Her aunt shrugged and at last gave way. "Though if I
didn't know Walter was only half flash and half foolish,
despite thinking himself top-of-the-trees, I wouldn't consider it for a moment. But it will do my soul good to turn
the tables on him, and you may be sure I will tell him a
few home truths when once I get my hands on him. It's
bringing you into it that I can't forgive, my love, and
though I daresay it's enterprising enough, and in fact
shows more gumption than I'd have given him credit for,
still, it's beyond what a body should be expected to bear.
And the sooner I am rid of him the better."

Sorrel couldn't help but laugh. "Dearest Aunt, you
talk as if you almost admire him for it. But if I am
right—and I think I am—Mr. Walter Granville need not
bother you ever again."

If Sorrel did not plan to enjoy herself quite as much as
she had made her aunt think, she was in truth glad to be
able to do something at last to help her aunt, and was,
besides, not in the least afraid of Walter, as she had said.

She had studied the letter and the map sent to her
aunt, and been relieved to see that the proposed rendezvous was at no great distance, in a wood that Sorrel
had ridden by on that abortive day so long ago. It was
also, she noticed grimly, the very wood where Walter
had taken the gentlemen to shoot; and no doubt he had

used the opportunity of noting a likely spot for his far less noble undertaking.

Noon was the appointed time, but Sorrel meant to get there well before then, for she hoped to catch Walter red-handed. If so, she meant to confront him immediately, and though she was not afraid of him, after some thought she went to the billiards room and took one of a set of dueling pistols she knew to be kept there. She did not mean to use it, of course, but it might alarm Walter sufficiently to make him admit the truth, and she had long ago become familiar with pistols and was herself a fairly good shot.

Besides, there was the slight chance that it was not Walter after all, in which case she would do as well to be armed.

On the appointed day she found the wood with little trouble, but its closely grown trees and thick undergrowth scarcely invited one to explore further. But then Walter was no doubt counting on that fact, for he would scarcely relish an audience for his retrieval of the money—or to risk someone getting there and finding it before he could come.

The going indeed soon became too rough to continue on horseback, and so with a shrug Sorrel dismounted, leading her horse and picking her way carefully through the tangle of briars and dead leaves and branches. Her goal was a clearing halfway through the wood, where she was to leave the money and depart. But of course it was only the first part of that directive she meant to obey. Afterward she meant to secrete herself in some convenient spot and wait for whoever came to pick the money up.

There was always the chance that Walter would send someone else of course. But somehow she did not think so. He must want as few people to know as possible, for he would be laying himself open to future blackmail attempts. And besides, knowing Walter, it was unlikely that he would trust anyone else to handle such a large sum. No, he would come himself.

It had been a sunny enough day when she started out, though with some threatening clouds in the distance. But once within the wood the canopy of trees grew so thickly overhead that the sun was quickly obscured. She soon found herself in an artificial twilight, which made the going even more difficult. Twice she had to stop and untangle the skirt of her riding habit from an encroaching bramble or thorn, and once she advanced unwarily and badly scratched her cheek on a projecting limb.

Touching the smarting scratch, she said an unladylike word or two, and firmly refused to regret her decision in coming. But the way soon became so rough that she was obliged to tie up her horse and leave him, trusting that he would not work his way free and leave her to walk the long way home. (Or worse, be discovered by Walter, when he came, and her advantage of surprise completely lost.)

Without that encumbrance the way was easier, certainly, and though the deeper she went into the wood the gloomier it got, she told herself firmly that that was merely because the sun's rays could not penetrate. Besides, she was certainly not afraid of the dark. In addition she was far too old to be flinching at shadows and imagining bogeymen behind every bush, even if the wood did look like the setting for every fairy story she had ever read.

She was thankful when she reached the clearing at last, with no more than a scratched cheek and a few scrapes to show for it. There some pale light penetrated, so that it seemed positively bright by comparison, and she looked around quickly and with her heart definitely beating a little faster in her breast. But she soon satisfied herself that no one lurked in the shadows, or deep in the wood on either side, watching her.

She had brought a tapestry bag with her that contained, not the ten thousand pounds the blackmailer had demanded, but a quantity of paper. That she carefully placed in plain view, and then retreated with some regret from the more cheerful clearing, and settled herself beneath the trees at some distance, while still close enough to see who came to collect the money.

Her dark habit was nearly invisible in the gloom, she knew, and she had chosen a spot in a more thickly concealing thicket than usual, so she felt safe enough. Despite that reassuring fact, her heart still beat a little faster for some few minutes, even though she knew it was some time still to the rendezvous time. Telling herself not to be a fool, she nevertheless carefully withdrew her pistol from the pocket of her skirt, and assured herself that it was primed and ready.

Chapter 19

But as the minutes wore on, Sorrel began to be amused at herself, for it soon began to seem that tedium, not fear, would be her greatest enemy. Soon her heartbeat had settled to its normal rate, and she began to try to make herself more comfortable for the long wait, thinking how absurd she would feel if he didn't show up at all, and she had gone through this elaborate charade for nothing.

So it began to seem, for the appointed time gradually crept up, and she saw nothing at all stirring, save for a few forest creatures who began to creep out and go about their daily affairs. She amused herself for some time watching a family of squirrels, who gamboled in the clearing and chased each other up trees.

After a while a jay came screeching through and drove them away, and Sorrel was left completely to her own devices. These were occupied wholly with her enterprise for some time, for though her earlier slightly heightened senses had been somewhat lulled by the long period of inaction, she still showed a tendency to start at every sound, and had nearly leapt up when the jay had erupted into the clearing, shattering the silence.

She was annoyed with herself over that, for if it had truly been Walter, she would have betrayed herself at once. She made herself watch more strictly for a while after that, but when it began to grow even darker, and the time dragged on, she began to think with longing of a warm fire and a comfortable chair. She was growing increasingly cold and uncomfortable.

While she had thought boredom was to be her chief challenge, in a very little while she was to discover unpleasantly that she had something far worse to contend with. In the deep woods it was a great deal cooler, of course, than the bright June day she had left without; and sitting on the damp ground for so many hours had made her distinctly chilly. But it soon became clear that the gloom of the wood had masked a change in the weather, for it shortly began to drizzle.

Under the canopy of trees she was somewhat sheltered, but occasional drops found themselves down to where she sat, and it grew a great deal chillier of a sudden. She turned up the collar of her habit and wished she had had the sense to bring a cloak with her, for at the very least she could have sat on it to protect her from the dampness of the ground.

She had not, however, so there was no use repining. She huddled closer to the trunk of a tree, seeking deeper shelter, and rechecked the priming of her pistol to make sure it did not get wet.

It seemed all right, and though she was strongly tempted at that point to give up, for Walter was very late, and retire from a hiding place that was growing momentarily more uncomfortable, she stiffened her backbone and would not be so weak and missish. Soldiers had often to sit and even sleep in far worse downpours than this, as she knew very well, and if they could ignore the moisture dripping uncomfortably down their necks, so could she.

William had been a sailor, of course, but they had squalls and worse to contend with. But Wycherly had been a soldier, though it was sometimes hard to remember that. He must have endured untold privations in the Peninsular War, for all soldiers did, and that had been a particularly bloody one.

She quickly jerked her mind from that dangerous

topic, and hugged herself to keep warm. Despite all she could do she was growing steadily colder and wetter. She was still more or less protected from the brunt of the rain, but enough seeped through to make her habit feel generally clammy, and her hands and feet were long since numb from the cold. She was tempted to get up and walk around a bit, stamping her feet to wake them up. But she feared as soon as she did, Walter would come and she would have revealed herself and frightened him off.

For the longer she waited in such miserable conditions, the more determined she grew to catch him in the act. Her aunt could then be free of him and she, Sorrel, could return home in peace.

She was a little startled to discover that she had, without being consciously aware of it, indeed made up her mind to return home as soon as she could do so without offending her aunt. She was not sorry she had come to England, and she had learned a great deal about her mother she had never known before. Besides, she was genuinely fond of Aunt Lela, and could never regret discovering her English relations.

But things were becoming ever more awkward with her English cousin, and there was a more craven reason as well. She discovered no wish in herself to stay and watch Livia married to the marquis, which if she remained much longer, she feared she would be trapped into doing. She had few illusions, and if his lordship was proving strangely dilatory—and making inexplicable advances where he should not—she had no real doubt that Livia would win out in the end. Parents might teach their daughters that virtue inevitably triumphed over mere shallow beauty; but that was for fairy tales only. In the real world those same parents were all too likely to be crowded around the latest beauty, while her plainer but more virtuous cousins sat in the corner unnoticed. And Sorrel drew the line at watching the marquis wed her spoiled cousin, knowing as she did that Livia would make him the worst possible wife.

Deliberately she again dragged her thoughts from such unproductive channels, and back to the business at hand. Walter, if he planned to come at all—and she had to acknowledge that perhaps the rain had prevented him—would have to come soon, or it would be completely dark. And she had no intention of remaining in the wood at night, despite her devotion to her aunt. But she could not believe that for ten thousand pounds he would allow a little rain to deter him. Nor could she believe he meant to let the money sit out alone all night, for though the wood was scarcely much frequented, and she had seen no one the whole long cold afternoon, she knew from inquiries that there was an abandoned woodsman's hut not too distant. Surely he would not risk his profitable marriage in such an outrageous attempt, and then not come to collect his illicitly obtained money.

It was growing steadily darker, and she was by that time thoroughly cold and wet and could scarcely feel her hands and feet any longer. But still she stubbornly remained in her frozen hiding place from moment to moment, unwilling to admit defeat. She had no doubt that a good deal of her stubbornness had to do with her reluctance to acknowledge that she had suffered such discomfort all in vain. But it was also in part because she had no desire to be obliged to return to her aunt and admit she had been wrong and they would have to start over again.

But she hadn't been wrong. She knew it. And Walter would come. He must.

When the first sounds reached her ears of someone walking quietly, even stealthily through the forest, her first emotion was quiet triumph. It was only immediately afterward that she felt the first flicker of fear that she could not quite disguise, even from herself.

But triumph quickly reasserted itself. He had come, like a fish to the fly, just as she had known he would!

She checked her pistol again, fearing that it had gotten too damp and would misfire (not that she had any intention of firing, of course, unless she had to), and rose stiffly to her knees, so she could see better. For a long while nothing happened, though the sounds still reached her, faint and scarcely discernible. At times she began to think she had imagined it, but then would come the faint snap of a twig, as if he had stepped unwarily, or the scrape of cloth against the underbrush. She knew too well how treacherous was the path, and grinned a little to herself in the gloom, thinking it served him right.

He was obviously being careful, though, which surprised her. If he smelled a trap he would be more wary, and possibly even more dangerous, though she still refused to be afraid of anyone so paltry as her aunt's third husband. Nevertheless she tightened her grip on her pistol, and got carefully and silently to her feet, trusting that it was dark enough that she would still be invisible.

Her feet protested, for they would seem to have gone wholly to sleep during her long surveillance, no doubt aided by the cold, for they felt like lumps of someone else's flesh. She was annoyed with herself for not having gotten up now and then to walk, for she knew from experience they would soon be shot through with painful pins and needles as the blood returned. Her hands, too, were numb, and slippery on the pistol. She shivered, partly from excitement, partly from cold, and tried to ignore these minor discomforts. For someone was definitely approaching the clearing, still with obvious wariness.

The next moment a dark figure had emerged from the deeper woods and looked around swiftly. It was too dark by then for her to make out his face but she thought it was Walter. She knew another quiet feeling of triumph and strained to better see what he was doing.

What he was doing was somewhat mysterious. He remained in the open clearing, looking around him sharply, and she could only suppose he wanted to assure himself that he was quite alone before he retrieved the money. He was dressed for riding, in buckskins and a dark coat, but at least he had had the sense to put on a cloak to protect him from the elements. It seemed very wet, which supported her suspicion that it was raining a great deal harder out from under the trees, which to some extent had mercifully sheltered her.

Still she remained where she was, for she wanted to catch him in the very act of taking up the tapestry bag, so there could be no question of his guilt. Excitement had thankfully stilled her shivers, and her many discomforts were completely forgotten for the moment. She scarcely dared breathe as she waited for him to indict himself beyond all hope of excuse, and as a last precaution, silently drew back the hammer of the pistol, as she had been so carefully taught.

And at last she was rewarded. He still seemed wary, but he went slowly to the place where the tapestry bag lay, by now quite wet, and bent to pick it up. He still seemed to be listening or waiting for something, but even as she watched he opened it up and looked inside.

She took an unwary step, meaning to emerge from her hiding place and confront him, the pistol held at the ready. But her frozen feet betrayed her. They had indeed proceeded to the pins and needles stage, and when she took a hasty step forward, her left foot crumpled completely underneath her.

She had a sharp moment of acute awareness before disaster struck. A twig cracked sharply under her leaden foot, inexorably betraying her, and the dark figure swung around sharply to face her. But even as she fell, her finger tightened unwittingly on the trigger of the pistol she was holding, already primed and cocked. There was a deafening explosion and as she watched in horror, the dark figure checked and was thrown back, and she knew that she had hit him.

But that was nothing to the sick terror that was still to come. As he had turned she had caught sight of his face clearly for the first time and knew it was not Walter at all.

It was the marquis.

She gave a hoarse cry she scarcely recognized as her own, and dropped the pistol where she stood as if it had burned her. Then she tore out of her hiding place and ran to him, uncaring if someone else might be watching. She dropped on her knees beside his still figure, lying ominously motionless on the wet slippery leaves of the clearing, terrified of what she would find, for she was certain that she had killed him.

"Oh, my God! What have I done?" she cried, frantically feeling for his heart. He was very wet, and still did not move, and had twisted a little, so that she could not get her hand underneath his wet coat. "Oh, God! I can't have killed him! I can't have!"

She was whimpering, scarcely knowing what she was saying, knowing only that it was by now too dark to see, even in the clearing, and that there the rain was falling very much harder. Even if he was not already dead, she could not hope to move him, and if she left him there in the rain he would undoubtedly die before she could get help to him.

And still he had not moved. His face was wet, his eyes closed, and he might be bleeding to death even then, but for some reason all her expertise in nursing had abandoned her. At the one time it had never mattered more, she was neither practical nor steady, for her hands trembled pitiably as she searched for a pulse, in a way that had nothing to do with the cold. And all the while she could only keep repeating sickly over and over again, "I've killed him. I've killed him. Oh, God, I've killed him."

Then a warm hand came up to cover her own, and his eyes opened a trifle quizzically, and he said in a perfectly natural voice, "You flatter yourself, my dear. You aren't that good a shot."

So sure had she been that she had killed him that for a moment she couldn't take it in. She could only stare at him as if he had been a ghost, and instead of feeling relief after the horrors of her earlier fears, she wanted quite desperately to burst into tears.

But that steadied her, for she had always been the one to be relied upon in an emergency. She managed to utter in a voice that sounded even less like her own, "Y-you're not dead—?"

He smiled at her with what she could only consider wholly insensitive cheerfulness. "You needn't sound so disappointed, sweetheart!" he said in amusement. "Are all Americans quite so bloodthirsty, or is this merely a hangover of the late war between our respective nations?"

She sat back on her heels, unaware of the rain pouring down upon her ruined hat and dripping off her face; still less able to believe that he really was alive and it was all not some figment of her horror and guilt. "I thought— oh, God, I thought I had killed you," she whispered. "What are you doing here, anyway? I thought you were—"

"Walter Granville, I know," he finished calmly for her. "Or at least I hope that was who you were aiming for, and the bullet wasn't actually meant for me. And don't look so astonished. When you didn't return, I eventually got the whole story out of your rather remarkable aunt. Which reminds me, I have a considerable bone to pick with you, Miss Kent."

That seemed to be putting the matter extremely mildly, under the circumstances. Sorrel could only continue to stare at him, feeling stupid, for her brain no longer seemed to work. "My *aunt* told you?" she repeated in disbelief.

"Eventually, as I said. She was quite as worried about you as I was, and I was finally able to—er—persuade her in the end to be frank with me. You might take a lesson from her, my dear Miss Kent!"

Chapter 20

When she still said nothing, he smiled at her in the charming way she had feared for one horrible instant never to see again. "My poor, foolish widgeon, I might have expected your aunt to behave in so bird-witted a manner, but I had insensibly come to expect better of you. You must have known I would neither be shocked nor particularly surprised to discover what your aunt's extremely inestimable husband was up to. It might interest you to know that Fitz has known him for years, and would be even less surprised, I gather. And don't look so bewildered. My poor misguided child, did you really believe me capable of packing my bags in disgust and removing myself immediately if I learned the truth? I am more than aware you do not trust me, but I thought you at least knew me better than that."

"No," she stammered, her teeth beginning to chatter, either from cold, or delayed reaction. "It was my aunt who w-would not have you told. She f-feared—"

"That I would not offer for her extremely beautiful and equally tiresome daughter if I came to hear of it," he finished for her again somewhat wearily. "I know that, too—and it is not often I have cause to so completely regret my own folly and misdirection, however born out of boredom it may have been. But edifying as this conversation may be—and as refreshing as it is to have you be open with me, at long last—I can think of better places for it to take place other than in the middle of a dark wood in the rain. Besides, it is more than time I got you home. You are shuddering with the cold, and little wonder. Had you no more sense than to sit out here in the rain?"

She wanted more than ever to weep, but she had to pull herself together. His tone, half caressing, half teasing—the things he called her—she would be a fool to make too much of them. And nothing had changed between them, after all. Nothing.

Nor did she yet understand at all what he was doing there. "B-but—I don't understand. W-why did you come? And where's W-Walter?" she managed, for her teeth were chattering in good earnest and she was almost shuddering from the cold.

He sighed. "Probably at home, warm and dry where he belongs—which is where I wish I had you. I must confess Walter's movements don't interest me very much at the moment. As for what I'm doing here, even though my experience of you has led me to feel sure you could deal with any number of blackmailers single-handedly, and you have made it more than plain that you mean to keep your adventures all to yourself, I thought I would just come along and see what was happening. Just a mopping-up operation, you know. And if you don't mind my saying so, it is as well I did. Really, I don't even mean to ask why you saw fit to bring a pistol along with you—for very little you did would surprise me any longer. But whatever possessed you to fire it? I don't mean to deny that your aunt would be a great deal better off without such a husband. But while you might have been able to hush up the scandal of your stepuncle's trying to blackmail your aunt, if you had succeeded in murdering him it would have been very much more difficult."

She was gradually regaining her wits, and feeling a little more herself. "Of course I didn't mean to kill him," she said indignantly. "The pistol went off by accident when I tried to move. My feet had fallen asleep and I tripped!" That brought back her earlier terror, however, and she said more anxiously, "In fact, I can't believe—I was sure that I had struck you!"

"Ah, it is always good to have such minor mysteries cleared up," he inserted, ignoring the latter question completely. "And if you have been out here all this time it is no wonder your feet went to sleep—and your hands are like ice. You absurd little fool, if you needs must lie in wait for blackmailers, had you no more sense than to come out without a cloak? It will be a miracle if you don't catch pneumonia, sitting all these hours in the rain. Come. As I said, it is more than time I got you home. Besides, your aunt will be worrying. I left her torn between coming in search of you yourself, and sending for the local justice of the peace, so you may judge how worried she was. Besides, you may be too frozen to notice by now, but this ground is deucedly wet and I'm tired of sitting upon it."

But when he attempted to rise he grimaced, though he did his best to hide the fact from her. She was not fooled, however, and said in rising certainty, "You're hurt! I knew I had hit you! Where? How bad is it?"

He grimaced again, and ruefully put a hand to his left arm. "Well, you needn't boast of it. You did succeed in winging me, however, if that makes you feel any better. I daresay I'm lucky the pistol went off by accident and you weren't indeed aiming to kill me, or I make no doubt I would be dead by now. There seems to be no end to your accomplishments, Miss Kent."

She scarcely paid attention to his nonsense, having discovered by then the long rent in his left sleeve, which was covered with blood. Her hands were trembling pitiably and she was scarcely in a state to think rationally, but the sight somehow managed to steady her, for it was at least something concrete. Her training stood her in good stead, and she was able to determine with profound relief that it was indeed no more than a flesh wound, and not serious. "We are not going a step until I have bound up this arm," she said firmly. "I don't think it is serious—you are indeed lucky I was not aiming at you, for I am an excellent shot!—but you are losing a lot of blood. I don't think the bone is broken—and there is not the least need to laugh. You will only make it bleed more!"

For he had gone off into paroxysms of laughter. "Oh, my incomparable Miss Kent! What a soldier's wife you would have made. I am even more sorry that I sold out. But I am quite sure my arm is not broken. I *am* bleeding like a stuck pig, however, for which I apologize. Bind it up with my handkerchief and let's get out of here. Much as I am enjoying this conversation—and as difficult as it is to get you on your own!—I really think there are better locations for it."

He endured her binding both their handkerchiefs tightly around his arm in a tourniquet, but would not hear of her fashioning a sling for it. "My dear, I am a good deal harder to kill than you seem to believe. It is the veriest scratch, I tell you."

She suspected the wound was more painful than he let on, but she was more concerned with getting him in out of the rain at the moment. Her suspicions were confirmed when she helped him up and he swayed a little, before he steadied himself. "Thank you. I left my horse with your own, but I'm afraid it will take us a considerable amount of time to find them in this light, and you are soaked and shivering already. Devil take it! This is growing less amusing by the moment," he admitted. "I don't suppose you would consent to remain here and let me bring the horses to you?"

She reacted with scorn to that suggestion, and he conceded ruefully, "No, I didn't think so. Spoiled beauties like your cousin occasionally have their virtues, I must confess. But don't you mean to take the bag of money back? I was just investigating it when I was—er—distracted."

"Good Lord, there's no money in the bag!" she said in

astonishment. "You don't think I would be so foolish as to risk carrying all that money around with me, do you?"

He laughed even more immoderately at that, which encouraged her to fear that he was becoming light-headed. But he insisted on wrapping his own cloak about her before they started out, and in the end she was forced to give in in the interests of time. She already knew how stubborn he could be, and the mulish set of his jaw encouraged her to believe that he would not stir a foot until he had his way.

He further refused to lean on her as they made their way back rather blindly through the treacherous undergrowth. The way had been difficult enough in daylight, but in the rain and darkness it was doubly bad. But at least she had to admit he walked steadily enough, and even insisted on going ahead of her through the worst of it, sheltering her as much as he could from the wet and whipping branches.

Even with his help the short trip seemed endless. She feared that for all his bravado he was hurt more than he let on, and she herself was cold, miserable, and frightened.

But worse was to come. When they reached the spot where she was sure she had tied up her own horse, and where he said he had left his as well, there was no sign of one, let alone two horses.

At first she could only think she must have mistaken the place in the dark, but he said slowly, "No, this is it, all right. Apart from the fact that I noted it well, there are signs that horses have been here recently. I am finding this of a sudden much less amusing, I must confess!"

His voice sounded strained, and she said woodenly, with another fearful glance at him, "Well, they are not here now. And you can obviously not walk all the way back, whatever you are about to insist to the contrary! It doesn't matter. I was told there is an abandoned woodsman's cottage not far from the clearing. At least there we can get in out of the rain and I can attend to your arm properly."

He, too, glanced at her rather sharply in the dark, but then said, "It seems you never cease to amaze me. Very well, let us find this abandoned cottage of yours, my dear."

The walk back was even worse, perhaps because they had no promise of warm clothes and a hot meal at the end of it. She was by then too worried about him to have much time to spare for her own wretched state. It took them a long, wearisome time to find the abandoned cottage, and though he remained upright and cheerful to the last, she could not help but fear that he was concealing the worse from her. It might be no more than a scratch— indeed she profoundly hoped so—but he had lost a good deal of blood, and this walk was doing him no good whatever.

They were both so wet by then it was impossible to be any wetter or colder, but she had his cloak as well. She doubted it would do any good to insist he take it back, and so she plodded steadily on, being struck in the face by cold wet branches when he was too slow to protect her, fear and guilt an ever-present accompaniment.

They almost literally ran into the cottage when they found it, for it was tiny and showed no lights, and was situated where the forest encroached on every side. Even in daylight it must have been dark and gloomy. In the cold and wet it scarcely looked much of a haven.

Even so she was relieved beyond measure to have found it. They struggled around and found the door, latched but thankfully not locked against intruders. Sorrel was the one to release the latch, and together they almost fell through the door, staggering like a pair of drunken lovers.

Inside, though they were indeed out of the rain, it was scarcely any better. It was pitch black, and smelled damp and stale, and seemed for some reason even colder than it had been outside. Her heart sank, for aside from every other consideration, she must see more thoroughly to his arm, and it was hardly the place to tend a gunshot wound. The place was probably filthy, and she had every reason to fear both infection and the ever-present threat of fever, the chances of both of which could only be made worse by his being thoroughly wet and chilled to the bone, as she had every reason to know he was. Worse, it was all her fault. If he died from an inflammation of the lung or from losing too much blood, she would have killed him.

But the marquis straightened and spoke cheerfully, as if their desperate trek through the dark and rain had been nothing out of the ordinary, and their proposal to take shelter in an abandoned cottage in the woods the merest commonplace. "Ah! Couldn't be better. Once we get a fire going, it will soon be warm enough."

"Will it?" she asked hollowly, trying hard to keep the tremor out of her voice. "*If* we get a fire started, you mean. All the wood must be wet, and if appearances are anything to go by, it's been a very long time since anyone lived here. Probably the chimney is blocked with nests and pine needles."

"Come, you don't mean to lose heart on me now, do you?" She could hear the smothered laugh in his voice, which at least made her hope he was not about to expire from loss of blood. "Believe me, I have slept in many worse in Spain. Good Lord, we are in the lap of luxury, for I've spent more nights than I care to remember in a far ruder hut, with nothing but a mud floor and a hole in the ceiling to let the smoke out. We shall soon be snug enough, I promise you."

She began to perceive that even yet she did not know him, for it was obvious she only knew the elegant marquis, not the seasoned campaigner that he must have been. But his determined optimism made her feel ashamed of her own weakness, and she determinedly straightened her spine. "Then we have no time to lose. I still have to clean your wound, and I must have light and a fire and some hot water, and warm dry cloths if we can manage them."

She thought he dropped a kiss on her wet curls, though she could not quite be certain. "Bless you," he said. "That's my girl! But as for hot water and warm cloths, you may have them certainly, but I told you I am much hardier than you suppose. Good Lord, if I didn't die when I was once wounded far worse than this and spent a night in a ditch filled with water, hiding from the French, I shan't die from a little scratch such as this. In fact, if you want to know the truth, I am enjoying myself far more right now than I have since I sold out."

That at least made her say a little scornfully, "Why, how could I have doubted it? My aunt should have thought of this when she was struggling to think how to entertain you. Little did she know that in place of dinner parties and balls, you required nothing but a hole in your shoulder and a cold and filthy cottage to sleep in, and you would be as merry as a grig."

He laughed. "Something very like, I will confess." He had managed to strike a flame from his tinderbox, and now looked about assessingly. For her part she thought the place looked even worse now that she could see it, for it was indeed filthy and all but empty, the few windows it possessed boarded over and the fireplace long since cold and with nothing but a few ashes left.

But he seemed not to find it in the least dispiriting, for he managed to light a spill, which provided them with a faint but more reliable light, and now pulled up the one remaining rickety chair with a flourish. "Now, Miss Kent, if you will consent to be seated here before the fire, I shall endeavor to show you just how comfortable our quarters may be."

But that was too much. "You shall do nothing of the sort. You should be the one to sit down. I'll get the fire started, and then I must see to your wound."

She had seen that martial light in his eyes once or twice before. "Yes, I know well that Miss Sorrel Kent of

America is everyone's support and comfort except her own. But it is time you accepted that I am not in the least like the others. You are cold and wet and despite all your bravery, still suffering from a certain amount of shock, and it is time someone took care of you for a change. Now sit down, there's a good girl, and let me have no more foolish arguments from you."

She sat, quite meekly for her.

Chapter 21

But her unwonted docility was only temporary. "But—"
He took her cold hands in his surprisingly warm
ones, and said patiently, "No buts. You may dress my
wound once we have both gotten warmed. I have let you
keep your absurd adventure to yourself because I was
foolish enough to want you to come to trust me. But now
I am in the saddle, and it is time you learned to do as
you're bid once in a while. Now drink this. Once I have
gotten the fire started we may try to figure out how to
get you properly warm."

She started to protest again, for among everything else
she had no desire for any more of his brandy. That was
what had gotten her in trouble in the first place. But she
took one look at his face and even more meekly sipped
at it, shuddering at the taste of the raw spirits. But she
could not deny that it was pleasant for once in her life to
have someone take care of her.

"That's my girl," he said approvingly, and again
dropped a kiss upon her hair. Then he laughed. "Don't
make such a face at my excellent brandy! I know well
you don't like it, but it will do a good deal toward warming you."

She had begun to think that task impossible, for she
had never been so cold before. But she feared she was in
considerable danger, not from a chill, but from reading
far more into this ludicrous situation than he perhaps intended, and so she made herself say firmly, "I will obey
you—for the moment. But we shall need the brandy later

to dress your arm. Besides, if I drank all this I should be regularly castaway."

He sighed with exaggerated patience. "I keep on telling you that you did no more than graze me. As for being castaway, I begin to think that might be a good idea, if it will make you more amenable to following orders. If one of my subalterns had questioned me and contradicted me as you are doing, I would have had him court-martialed on the instant. Now do as you're bid and we shall get on very much better, I promise you."

He was gone on the words, back out into the rain. She should protest that he was unfit, and insist upon doing it herself, but instead she sipped at her brandy again, finding that he was right, and its warmth was beginning to spread outward. Whether or not he was aware of it, he had uttered magical words. For some reason he seemed not to know or care that she was not a delicate helpless creature, like her mother or her cousin, to be helped over the least obstacle and guarded as if she were infinitely precious. But it was nice to be thought so, however briefly. Soon enough he would remember that she was practical and woefully unfeminine, and fully capable of taking care of herself, and realize his error. But it was unexpectedly tempting while it lasted.

But he showed no immediate signs of realizing the truth. He was back quickly with a load of firewood, and she had to admit that he managed to get a fire going out of such wet wood with a skill that she could not have hoped to equal. But he was favoring his left arm slightly, and she feared his activity had caused it to bleed again.

Once the fire was going to his satisfaction, he stood up and dusted off his hands, and said matter-of-factly, "Now, we must consider what is to be done to get you dry."

But there was a limit to her newfound docility, and she countered just as firmly, "On the contrary, now we must see how bad your wound is and dress it."

He cast her an amused look, but unexpectedly submitted without further protest to having his jacket eased off and his sleeve rolled up to lay bare the wound. Sorrel saw with great relief that it was indeed little more than a scratch, but said in disapproval, "As I feared, you have succeeded in making it bleed again. It needs to be cleaned thoroughly and bound up again, and I have no doubt a surgeon would say you should be bled. We must send for one the minute we get back tomorrow. And even then we will be lucky if you do not succumb to a high fever."

"Nonsense! From this little scratch? As for being bled, a surgeon might be so dotty-headed as to suggest it—I have been mauled about by enough ghoulish sawbones to believe anything of them!—but you may be sure he would never get close enough to me to get the chance. Besides, I have complete faith in your skills as a nurse. Bind it up and let's be done with it! And by the way, I hope you observe *my* meekness in this case, my dear Sorrel, and mean to take a lesson from me."

It seemed the brandy had done her good, for she was quite recovered by now. "If you mean to call it meekness to counter all my orders and refuse to listen to my advice, I do not!" she retorted, working busily. "Recollect I have a good deal of experience at dressing wounds, and I know what I'm talking about. Does that hurt?" she asked anxiously, as he flinched when she used the brandy to clean the wound.

"No, not a bit," he lied manfully. "You must tell me about your nursing, someday. I would like to hear of it."

She ignored that, and wrapped a strip torn from her petticoat—which was as dry a garment as she possessed at the moment—as tightly about his arm as she dared. He protested that she was making it too large for him to put his coat on again, and she countered, "You are not going to put your coat on again. You are going to put your arm in a sling that I am going to devise for you, and that is final. Remember I trust in your meekness in this matter."

He laughed. "Touché. But you are at least right that I am not going to put my coat back on again, for you must have it. It is less damp than that habit of yours, and unless I mean to see you with a high fever by tomorrow, we must get you warm and dry. I would like to strip you completely, but I don't aim at the moon. I have submitted to your decrees. Now it is your turn."

She tried in vain to argue that her habit would soon dry, but he was adamant. He made her strip off her wet jacket and put his own about her, then insisted on pulling off her muddy boots and rubbing her hands and feet briskly to get the circulation going again. It was the sort of service her mother—or her cousin—would have taken as their right. But she found it embarrassing, and feared the color in her cheeks betrayed her. Still, it was a new experience to be so tenderly taken care of, and he seemed not yet to have realized how unnecessary it all was.

He made her sit close to the fire, which was going nicely by then, and said ruefully, "Some rescue this has been. If I had been at all prepared, I should have brought some food and blankets with me. For despite the brave front you are putting on, I fear we shall both be deucedly cold by the morning."

"No, indeed. I am warming nicely, thanks to your fire—which I confess I could never have built half so well. I hope you see how docile I am being." She was, in truth, growing surprisingly sleepy as she warmed, so that it was becoming an effort to keep her eyes open.

He looked down at her in amusement, as if he realized it. "Deceptively docile. I fear it cannot last. I also fear my company cannot be as stimulating as I had hoped, for you are yawning most impolitely Miss Kent! Never mind. To bed with you! I've no liking for so sleepy a companion, and you will be the better for a good night's sleep."

She looked in wonder, and saw that he had made a bed of sorts before the fire from piled branches spread with his hastily-dried cloak. She opened her mouth to protest, for he was the one in need of the good night's sleep, but he had evidently expected it and forestalled her. "Don't argue! I will do very well on the floor, for I have spent many a night thus, I assure you."

She saw in his face that it would indeed do no good to argue. And so she submitted to lying down upon his makeshift bed, which proved surprisingly comfortable.

He went down upon one knee beside her to pull a corner of the cloak over her. In the firelight his face showed amusement, and something else that she dared not try to identify. "I might have known I could rely upon your intelligence, if not your fierce American independence. And you, Miss Sorrel Kent, are a woman among thousands. Nay, millions. Little as you seem to know it or realize it."

But since she was already drifting to sleep, under the effects of her tiring day and his strong brandy, she thought, but could not be sure, that he added under his breath, "And I thank God I am not stranded with your beautiful but pea-witted cousin!"

Much to her amazement, despite the cold and the hard bed, she slept soundly for hours.

She woke some time later, to find herself shivering with the cold, and the room much darker. She also realized that she was alone, and that the marquis was no longer in the room.

She started up with alarm, but almost immediately the door opened, and he came in, brushing off the raindrops and carrying a new load of wood.

She felt immediately guilty that he should be up tending to the fire when he was the one who was hurt, and murmured groggily, "I must have slept harder than I thought. Let me do that. You should not be required to shoulder all the responsibilities."

"I was hoping you would not wake to argue with me again!" he said in amusement. "Besides, mine is the blame, for I must have dozed off and let the fire go almost out. That's why it is so cold in here. But it shall soon be built up again. Go back to sleep. I'm sorry I wakened you."

He was right, for shortly the room began to grow warmer again. But instead of lying back down, she sat up and wrapped her arms around her bent knees, watching him build up the fire and perform other small tasks with a grace and economy of movement she found it a pleasure to watch. It seemed the noble marquis was but a disguise, and this was indeed the real man, capable and unfazed by conditions that would make Mr. FitzSimmons, for instance, blanch. She had indeed underestimated him.

He glanced around, as if aware of her eyes on him, and raised his brows. "Can't you sleep? Are you too cold?"

"No, toasty warm," she murmured sleepily. "Did you sleep at all?"

"For hours," he said cheerfully. He hesitated, then added, "But since we are both awake, and I seem to have had precious little opportunity to talk to you, tell me about America. I would like to hear of your country."

She was surprised. "Now?"

"Why not? We both seem to be awake. And you never talk about your home, you know. Or much of anything else for that matter. You seem to be content to sit and let others take all the attention."

"In my corner, I know!" she said a little resentfully. She did not need to be reminded she was scarcely scintillating company. But even so, it seemed somehow natural there, in the dark, with nothing but the firelight flickering, to say things she would never have said in the daytime. "America? It is not like England, I can tell you that. But I don't know how to describe it to you. It is young and raw and—exciting. Not like here, where everything is settled and peaceful and so—so ordered and civilized. Don't misunderstand me. England is beautiful. But so is my home, only in a different way."

"You live in Annapolis, don't you?"

"Yes. It is the capital of the state, and so we have a new domed state building, and many fine houses. But it is still very small and new compared with London. Even Washington, which is not far away, could never compare to London in size or sheer number of people and buildings. But America is—cozy, and far less hedged around with rules and etiquette and codes of conduct."

She could hear his laugh even though she was not watching him. "I would never have considered America cozy, with its Indians and revolutions. Most English, like your Lady Smythe, consider it quite barbaric and dangerous. But there must be a satisfaction in carving a new land out of the wilderness and having to fend for yourself."

She was again surprised at his words. "Yes," she said slowly. "At least, that was before my time, of course, and my grandfather used to tell me that all the excitement was gone, now. He was one of the Founding Fathers, you know, and fought in the revolution even though he was no longer a young man. It has always seemed odd to me that my grandfather should have fought against the English, and then my father married one."

"Not so odd. We are basically the same people, after all. But it seems to me not quite all the excitement has gone, for you have endured your own war, now. Tell me about it."

And so, there in the dark, and with no more prompting than that, she told him things she had not spoken of since, or thought to tell to another living soul. Of the time when the British navy sailed up the Chesapeake and fired on St. Michael's, when she and her mother had been sent to safety to their farm just outside the town. She told him of the way the guns had sounded all night, and how the citizens of the town had hung lanterns up in

the trees to fool the British, so that all of their rounds of
cannon went high, and missed the town completely.

He laughed at that, but said, "And what was the redoubtable Miss Kent doing all that time? Not sitting on
your hands, I imagine."

So she told him of the hysteria of most of the maids,
(and of her mother, too, if the truth be known, though
she did not tell him that) and how she had stationed the
few men still on the place with muskets to stand watch
all night, herself among them. For they had had no way
of knowing the fate of the town then, or if they might be
attacked, for all they could see and hear was the dreadful
sound of the British cannon, which had continued most
of the night.

He grunted at the end of that, and made no comment.
"And when Washington burned?" was all he asked.

That was even less pleasant to remember. The maids
had been in hysteria then, too, and her mama prostrated
by the vapors, for they had not known whether her father, who had been in the capital at the time, was alive or
dead. They could see the glow of it burning in the distance, and hear the cannon and the explosions then, too,
and so great was the light and heat that it almost seemed
the sun was rising in quite the wrong direction.

Then she had not been alone on a farm, of course,
with only a few boys and old men to rely upon. The
local militia had been called out, and there was much
fear that the British meant to burn all before them.

When she had finished, he was silent even longer.
And then he said almost reluctantly, "And the attack on
Baltimore? I understand you helped nurse the wounded
there."

That was something she still did not like to think
about, much less talk of. But then he more than anyone
must know what it had been like. And so she found herself telling him of that, too, and found some unexpected
relief in the telling.

Mama had refused to let her go, but for once Papa had

put his foot down, for he had been returned to them after the excesses of Washington, and knew what was likely to be happening. Other brave and determined women were going as well, and she had known she had to go, not simply because of William, who was stationed there, but because of all the others like William, whose wives and fiancées were too far away to help them. Her father himself had driven her toward Baltimore while the issue was still uncertain, and they had not known if the British had succeeded in taking Fort McHenry.

But the almost miraculous news that the fort had held, even against the assault of the famed British navy, was quickly eclipsed by the horrors they found there. She had not known such sights were possible, and if she had at the first been faint and sickened by the dreadful wounds and the smell and the groans of the dying, she had soon become too deadened to notice any longer. She had sponged wounds and held shattered limbs to be sawn off by the harried and exhausted doctors, and given drinks of water to poor, dying boys much younger than she was.

By the time she had found William, dying rapidly and painfully from a wound in the lower stomach, she had been beyond feeling. He had died in her arms, with a last smile and weak squeeze of her hand, and there had been no time for grief. Too many others still lay dying and needed her help. She had put his hand down almost automatically and gone on, unable to feel the grief she knew she should, and racked with guilt because of it.

After a long while, he said quietly, "You are indeed a heroine."

But she was uncomfortable with that. "I did no more than I had to. You must know that."

"Yes, I know that. But I also know that not everyone rises to the challenge as you did. What do you suppose your beautiful cousin would have done if faced with the same situation? Or your mother for that matter?"

But she was genuinely astounded. "But that is ridiculous. No one expects them to!"

"What can I do to make you understand?" he said in exasperation. "Not all men are obsessed by physical beauty. You underestimate yourself most shockingly, Miss Sorrel Kent."

But that was something he would never understand. At her continued silence, he sounded almost angry. "Instead you sit back and demand nothing. I only hope I may be present when you finally do discover what you want, my dear Sorrel. At least even your beautiful but tiresome cousin understands that you get little in this world without fighting for it, however beautiful or rich or advantaged you may be. For until that time I fear you will have to continue to content yourself with the dregs, as you have so obviously been doing. And that would be a shame, Miss Sorrel Kent. An almost criminal shame."

Then, before she could answer—if she could have found an answer to that cryptic statement—he had lifted his head and frozen for one moment. Then he said, in an entirely different voice, that sounded amazingly wrathful, "Hell and the devil confound it! Unless I miss my guess it's the rescue party. And if there was one thing I thought I could rely upon more than another, it's that my good friend Fitz could be trusted not to set out at dawn in this highly romantic but totty-headed fashion and ruin everything."

Chapter 22

The sounds of arrival were indeed unmistakable by then. Sorrel rose hastily, realizing she had scarcely noticed that dawn had arrived; and his lordship also rose, looking a trifle grim.

But they had not long to wait. Nor, it was soon apparent, did his lordship owe their early rescue to his totty-headed friend. For in a few moments the door opened, and to Sorrel's astonishment Livia tripped in, looking ravishing in the early morning light in a habit of blue velvet that exactly matched her eyes, followed closely by both Mr. FitzSimmons, and even more astonishingly, Aunt Lela.

Livia looked around at the dirty shack and drawled, "Well, well. Isn't this cozy?"

"Livia!" said her mother sharply. She then added to Sorrel with heartfelt sincerity, "My dear, I am so relieved to see you, alive and in one piece that I swear I could almost burst into tears right here! I was already blaming myself for having let you come, and I was downright relieved when his lordship tackled me and dragged the truth out of me. But when neither of you came back at all, and your horses showed up in the stables without you, I naturally feared the worse. I declare I was all for setting out in search of you at once, despite the hour and the fact I've seldom sat on a horse in my life. But Mr. FitzSimmons managed to prevail in the end upon my good sense, for I was forced to agree it would do you little good for us to get ourselves lost as well! But what happened?"

Sorrel was blushing a little by then, very aware of her disheveled state and the intimacy of the scene they had interrupted. But she said quickly, "Nothing. We were on our way back when we discovered our horses had disappeared. I supposed they must have managed to free themselves and galloped back to their warm stalls. But since it was so late we were obliged to put up here for the night."

"But did Walter come to pick up the money?" demanded her aunt.

"No. No one came, until his lordship. So it looks as if I may have been wrong after all."

"You weren't mistaken," said her aunt grimly. "And when I get my hands on him—"

But that was still another surprise for Sorrel. "Get your hands on him? Why? Where *is* Walter?"

It was Mr. FitzSimmons who answered. "No one seems to know, Miss Kent. He has disappeared, too."

"What?" his lordship asked sharply. "Granville has disappeared?"

FitzSimmons shrugged. "He was not in to dinner last night, and his bed seems not to have been slept in. In addition, some of his clothes are missing, along with his tilbury."

"Well, good riddance to bad rubbish, is what I say!" said Aunt Lela strongly. "I'm glad to be rid of him. Especially when I think how he risked my poor niece's life, and made me so unhappy, and embarrassed me in front of my guests! And now this! In the mood I'm in at the moment, even hanging is too good for him."

"Wait a moment, Mrs. Granville," begged the marquis. "Let me get this straight. Did you, in effect, pay him the ten thousand or any part of it that he allegedly demanded?"

"No, I did not! Catch me handing over any more to him to be thrown away on his horses and his gambling debts! If he wants to sue me, or create a scandal, why let him! I blame myself for letting all this get so far, and I have not slept a wink all night, fearing that something had happened to you or Sorrel."

"Why, that's very sensible of you," said the marquis. "But I'm still somewhat mystified. Do you tell me he fled without getting the money he had gone to such extraordinary lengths to obtain?"

"What's so mysterious about that? Belike he knew I was on to him, and feared facing me, as he'd every right to! To think of him writing me those nasty letters, and going about cutting girths and pushing over chimneys and such. Though now that I come to think of it, I can't quite see Walter capering over the roofs, but I suppose that's neither here nor there. No doubt he had an accomplice—probably one of those thatch-gallows friends of his! Well, he can stay away if he knows what's good for him."

"Wait a minute, Aunt Lela," said Sorrel, beginning to see what the marquis was driving at. "It does seem odd that he would go without obtaining his money. Did you say anything to him that might have hinted you were on to him?"

"Not unless he's better at reading the contempt in my eyes when they rested on him than I think, for he's never seemed to notice it before! But that must have been the reason. Why else would he have sneaked out as he did?"

"Oh, what does it matter?" demanded Livia impatiently. "I can't think what we are doing standing around in this filthy hovel! Let us go home, and then we can thrash it out to our heart's content, as we seem to have been doing ever since last night already."

But Mr. FitzSimmons had made an interesting discovery. "Hallo! What happened to you, old bean? Don't tell me Granville shot you on top of everything else?"

Aunt Lela exclaimed in horror as she, too, discovered the marquis's blood-spattered sleeve for the first time. But Lord Wycherly looked more than slightly annoyed.

"It's nothing. I was—er—checking that Miss Kent's pistol was in order, and it went off accidentally. A flesh wound, no more."

Mr. FitzSimmons grinned. "If that's your story, we'll stick to it, old lad. But I think it's one your army friends would certainly be interested to hear more of."

But the marquis successfully frowned him down. "Never mind that! But I must admit that I, too, like Miss Kent, find this story somewhat—unaccountable. Granville goes to all the trouble to blackmail you, and arrange at least two near-fatal accidents involving Miss Kent, and then disappears without making any attempt to collect the money?"

"Aye, well it does sound unlikely, put like that!" conceded Aunt Lela. "But then, he always was one with an uncanny instinct for preserving his own hide."

"I must also agree it does sound fishy," said Mr. FitzSimmons. "But who else could it have been? I would have tended to disbelieve so highly outrageous a tale, but knowing Granville's reputation, I am perfectly ready to believe almost anything of him. And no one, I take it, showed up at all to pick up the alleged payoff?"

"No," said Sorrel slowly, her brow wrinkled in thought. "But you're right. Who else could it have been? Unless—"

She broke off and could not prevent herself from looking to where her cousin stood, looking exceedingly beautiful and bored. In the pause, Livia said even more impatiently, "What does it matter who it was? My cousin is safe and Mama still has her ten thousand. If we must rehash it all over again, pray let us go somewhere else to do it."

Sorrel could not speak, for the suspicion that had just flooded her mind was too monstrous to be given credence, much less spoken. She did not realize that the marquis was watching her, or that Aunt Lela, too, had turned suddenly pale.

For she was wrestling with her own avalanching

doubts. It could not be true. She would not let herself believe it. It was too preposterous, and there could be no reason for it anyway. She must be mistaken.

When no one spoke, Livia went up to the marquis and put her hand on his arm and smiled up intimately at him, looking beautiful and incredibly fragile in her deep blue habit. "And I should think you would have had enough of this place, too, my lord. Imagine being obliged to spend the night here. You must be longing for a bath and some clean clothes, and a doctor should be sent for to look at your arm. I can't think what Mama is doing keeping you standing around here, or dragging you into her foolish troubles for that matter. I fear what you must think of us."

But something, whether it was the sight of her hand on his arm, or the way she so obviously expected her beauty again to get her exactly what she wanted, or even the slightly contemptuous, slightly patronizing glance she darted at her cousin, undoubtedly unkempt after having slept all night in her clothes, made something snap in Sorrel at last. She had not wanted to believe it, but suddenly it was crystal clear to her, and she blurted out before she could prevent herself, "*You!* It was you all the time!"

There was a frozen moment when Livia looked suddenly a great deal less beautiful. And then the marquis said quietly, "Bravo, my dear! Will you marry me?"

Livia gasped. "Now I see what this is all about!" she said bitterly. "I knew you were trying to steal him from me, but I never dreamed you would go this far. You must have thought you were clever, forcing him into spending the night with you, when all your earlier attempts to attract his attention failed. But do you think anyone will believe your wild accusations for one moment?"

The marquis carefully removed her hand from his arm. "There is no question of 'stealing me' from you, Miss Morden. I may have made the mistake of admiring your beauty when first we met, and in a fit of boredom and disillusion thought you would suit me as well as anyone else. But that was before I met your quite extraordinary cousin, and realized what a mistake I would have been making. And I must tell you I fully believe Miss Kent's accusations against you, for I had come to the same conclusion long before your too-trusting cousin."

But Sorrel could still scarcely believe it. "But why? Why would she do such a thing?"

"To drive you away, I suspect," he said calmly. "Didn't you know she has been jealous of you from the beginning, long before I came?"

"Of me? Jealous of me?" repeated Sorrel in disbelief.

"Certainly of you. You have wits and courage and strength of character, all of which she lacks. I realize you underestimate yourself shockingly, sweetheart, but in any other company but that of your cousin—or your mother, I gather—you would count as quite a pretty girl. But I began to despair that you would ever stand up to her and see the truth for yourself."

"But—but—" At last she looked at her aunt. What she saw there made her go to her quickly. "Dearest Aunt, don't look like that. It can't be true. I won't believe it."

But her aunt straightened her shoulders and said with her usual bluntness, "It's true, all right. I can see his lordship's right. It's my fault, I daresay, for never denying her anything. His lordship's also right that you're worth a dozen of her, beauty or no, and I've seen that as well. I just didn't want to admit it. In fact, I began to suspect long ago it was you he was interested in, not Livy, but I didn't want to acknowledge that either. It was only when you threatened to go home and start a school, and I began to see how unhappy you were looking, that I admitted the truth to myself. I hope you will be able to forgive me, my dear, for despite my blindness I'd never have sat still and let her risk your life the way it seems she has. Not Walter but my own daughter. Whether or not you can ever forgive me, I shall never forgive myself."

Sorrel hugged her convulsively. "Don't, Aunt! Don't think of it. Of course it is not your fault."

Her aunt patted her a little blindly and put her away. "That's like you, my dear. Perhaps Mr. FitzSimmons will be so kind as to escort us home again. I confess I am not feeling too well."

No one, least of all Sorrel, had looked at Livia for some time. Now Sorrel lifted her head and did so, seeing the defiance and the fury in her face, seeing that Livia had indeed done it and did not in the least regret it. Seeing, too, what she should have guessed long ago: that her cousin hated her. But of her famous beauty, that had caused Sorrel so much heart sickness and so much jealousy, there was very little evidence left.

Even Mr. FitzSimmons did not quite look at her as he took his hostess's arm, and led her out the door. But he did look back at his friend and grimace. "I daresay you won't be needing us. I can't yet thank you for this, but I daresay you've saved me from a fate worse than death. Damn you!" and he closed the door behind them.

Sorrel was left alone with his lordship, feeling remarkably shy.

After a moment he remarked prosaically, "Don't look so tragic, love. And don't waste your pity on her. If not Fitz, she will soon attach some other poor fool, for she *is* exceptionally beautiful."

"I envied her!" she said wonderingly. "Now I think it is her beauty that made her what she is. How could I have been so blind."

He grimaced as Fitz had. "You are more charitable then I can yet be. The only thing I can forgive her for is having thrown us together, however unwittingly. For she did, you know. Without her plots against you, it's very likely I would never have become acquainted with you, determined as you were to blend into the wallpaper. And

that doesn't bear thinking of! Just think. If I hadn't rescued you that first day, and you hadn't raked me down
for my title, and then smiled at me and completely
bowled me over, I might actually have ended up married
to your amoral cousin, and that bears thinking of even
less. Which reminds me. You still haven't answered my
question."

"Wh-what question?" She was breathless, and shy,
and hope was beginning to burgeon in her like a butterfly that had been too long in its chrysalis. For that was
exactly what she was.

He smiled down at her in the way she had come to
love and took her hand and said formally, "Miss Kent, I
realize that the customary thing is for me to speak to
your father and get his permission to pay my addresses
to you. But since he is thousands of miles away, and I
don't think you care any more for such nonsense than I
do, I am asking you to become my wife."

She met his eyes and searched them seriously, and did
not immediately give him an answer. "But you did mean
to offer for my cousin. Were you in the least in love with
her?"

He took her hand and carried it to his lips. "My love, I
will confess I came with some such purpose—though
you quickly drove it completely out of my head. I was
bored, and I will admit I was bowled over for a while by
her beauty. Besides, she seemed preferable to the snobbish aristocrats who were casting out lures to me for the
sake of my title, and I liked her mother."

Sorrel almost gasped at that. "But she only wanted to
marry you because of your title!"

"I know she did. But at least she made little attempt to
conceal the fact from me. I have no excuse, except that,
like you, I was at a point in my life where I didn't know
what I wanted, except for what I could not have, and
where I was going next. But even if you had not been
here to serve as a delightful contrast to your beautiful
but empty-headed cousin, with your quiet courage and

independent spirit, I can assure you that a few days spent in more close proximity with her would soon have convinced me of my mistake. I am only glad that Fitz has seen the truth before it is too late, for I believe he was genuinely in love with her. And still you have not answered my question."

She was growing instantly more sure of herself—and more beautiful. But still she held him off. "I am an American. I don't believe in titles and such outmoded privilege. Have you forgotten that?"

"I have forgotten nothing. Have I told you I adore you, my little democrat? If you can bear to become a marchioness, despite all your principles, I promise you we shall spend part of every year in America. I am longing to see it for myself, and suspect I shall feel very much at home there. Unfortunately, we cannot neglect my responsibilities here, but for a start, I thought we might buy Campden House and bring it back to life. That is in the way of a bribe, by the way, for despite everything, I still am damnably unsure of you. There have been a few times in the past week that I have managed to convince myself you are not indifferent to me, but the devil's in it I can't be sure of anything where you are concerned. So, for the third and last time, will you marry me, my independent little American?"

"Yes," she said simply.

And then she was in his arms, held so tightly that she couldn't breathe, and there was no more talk for a very long time.

It was only long afterward, when he had lifted her onto her horse and they were riding back together slowly, their hands locked together, that she thought to ask in mystification, "But what do you suppose became of Walter?"

He laughed. "I don't know, and I must confess I don't care. He was talking of slipping off to some race meeting that he knew your aunt wouldn't approve of. I suspect it is too much to expect that she will be rid of him so easily."

"Poor Aunt Lela," she said, sobering momentarily.

His hand tightened on hers, and a hot look came into his eyes again; reminding her of those earlier breathless moments. She returned the pressure and smiled at him, not even wondering any longer how so handsome and charming a man could be in love with her.